A MULTILINGUAL DECAMERON

Stories of a different world

SCHOOL OF LANGUAGES AND APPLIED LINGUISTICS

THE OPEN UNIVERSITY

Project team

This book was conceived and compiled by Anna Comas-Quinn, María Fernández-Toro, Lina Adinolfi, Caroline Tagg and Emilia Wilton-Godbertforde, with the invaluable help of Kim Downs and Hannah Kemp.

Editorial support was provided to the authors by language specialist editors Zhiqiong Chen, Anna Comas-Quinn, María Fernández-Toro, Clare Horáčková, Vicki Lywood-Last, Esther Santos Grimaldos, Birgit Smith, Piero Toto, Emilia Wilton-Godbertforde and Karine Zbinden.

The book was edited and the cover designed by Michelle Lawson.

Contents

· Day three ·

Preface

This project, **A Multilingual Decameron**, was inspired by the medieval Italian writer Boccaccio's *Decamerone* (1353), a fictional work of 'novelle' (short stories). The 'novelle' were set during the 1348 epidemic of the Black Death in Florence, when ten men and women confined themselves to a villa in the hills outside the Italian city for ten days and entertained one another by telling stories. The onset of the Covid-19 global pandemic in early 2020 prompted several communities to recreate the Decameronian experience in modern times by writing and sharing stories to raise morale during confinement.

The stories featured in this volume were written by students taking courses in the languages taught at the Open University, UK. At a time where personal, academic and professional lives were being disrupted by the pandemic, the aim of the initiative was to bring these students together by drawing on the wealth of multilingual and multicultural resources that are key assets of this diverse learning community. The initiative also sought to encourage the students' creativity and sense of ownership over the different languages within their repertoire. They were therefore invited to draw fully on their available linguistic resources in order to express themselves, including combining elements from more than one language or from different varieties of the same language.

In editing the stories, it was not our intention to produce native-like versions of the original manuscripts. Rather, we aimed to preserve the freshness and authenticity of students' own voices and include their level of proficiency in the languages they adopted. Thus, while we took care to correct spelling, punctuation and grammar errors, we deliberately retained some unusual word choices and turns of phrases in the contributions to the volume.

Inevitably, some languages feature more prominently than others. This reflects the demographic make-up of our student population and their varying levels of confidence using different languages. To help you appreciate the writers' linguistic trajectories, the languages that they consider to be their 'home languages' are indicated at the end of each contribution.

The theme for the book is **'A different world'**, allowing for many diverse interpretations by the authors. Thus, you will find fictional stories alongside autobiographic ones, ranging from factual accounts to surreal experimentations. Most stories are written as prose but a few are written as poems. Some reflect on lockdown as a strange new world, while others conjure up different scenarios, drawing on early childhoods, fantastic imagined futures, and everything in between. Inspired by the fourteenth century *Decameron*, the stories are divided into ten days, each of which includes ten to twelve contributions. Instead of grouping them thematically we tried to mix topics and languages as much as possible to help the reader experience their sheer variety.

We hope you enjoy reading this unconventional collection of stories and that you find the contributors' creation of different worlds in difficult times entertaining, thought-provoking, comforting, and inspiring.

· Day one ·

The language of love

Barbara Bonatti Divers

My mother passed away last week, and on my return today, I found two letters of condolences from her long-standing residents, Herr Ullmann and Madame Joubert. I am pleased and a little puzzled, I figure they must both be over eighty by now…

You see, for many years my mother ran a Pensione near the Adriatic coast. Her place offered a gentle sea-breeze all year round, a secluded bay nearby, and the proximity to essential amenities without the madding crowds of popular resorts. Some elderly holidaymakers kept coming back from Germany and France, and a few ended up staying for most of the year. This never ceased to amaze me, since my mother could only speak Italian.

I remember helping out at the Pensione during my school holidays and trying to pick up a few words, like 'Bonjour', 'Danke', etc. Mostly, though, my communication technique consisted of a flurry of nodding and gesturing. Not my mum's, however. She used to look serenely into old schoolmaster Ullmann's troubled eyes, waiting patiently for him to finish speaking in German. Then she would nod sagely, respond in two or three thoughtfully constructed Italian sentences, and send him on his way – looking strangely reassured, if a little dazed. «*Che voleva, mamma*?» I would ask – what did he want? «*Soltanto un orecchio, cara*» – just an ear, darling, she would reply with a little smile (leaving me to picture her lopsided!) before asking me to help her make her famous apricot tart.

With Madame Joubert, who came originally from Lyon, things were stranger still. I caught her and my mum in the herb garden a few times, working together and talking to each other intimately – my mother in Italian and Mme Joubert in French – with no apparent need for an interpreter… «*Una donna simpatica,* we have a lot in common» my mum would say by way of explanation, when questioned about it.

„*Meine liebe Clara"* reads Herr Ullmann's letter „*Mit deiner Mutter habe ich einen Teil meiner Seele verloren. Sie wusste immer, was ich brauchte, bevor ich es tat. Manchmal war ich über etwas beunruhigt und sie würde es wissen und meine Lieblings-Aprikosentarte machen … Ah, die himmlische Tarte!"*…so her famous apricot tart was her way to give Herr Ullmann affection at difficult times…

« *Ma chère Claretta* » are Madame Joubert's words « *Ta mère était la seule véritable amie avec qui je pouvais parler de tout. Elle m'a toujours comprise, tandis que les autres ne me comprenaient pas* » … In the envelope she has put a few sprigs of lavender that have brought back memories of my mother's herb garden.

This, I now understand, was her secret: her ability to empathise, to care about others sincerely, to give them what they needed instinctively. Language, for her, was never a barrier. «*Ricordati, tesoro*» – remember, darling, she told me once «*chi parla vuole essere ascoltato. E se ascolti, avrai già aiutato*» – those who speak wish to be listened to. And if you listen, you have already helped.

Barbara's home languages are Italian and English.

La vida después de COVID19: el cuento de un viajero

Christine Kass

El mundo cambió para mí en diciembre de 2019. Llevaba seis años viviendo y enseñando inglés en China. A pesar del choque cultural, aprendí rápidamente a amar este país y, además, me dio la oportunidad de viajar a todos los países con los que había soñado: Japón, Vietnam, Camboya, entre otros. Realmente fue una experiencia maravillosa.

De repente la experiencia bonita desapareció. Cuando las noticias del COVID-19 aparecieron por primera vez, no les presté mucha atención. Sin embargo, después de unos días me di cuenta de lo grave que era la situación, pues comenzaron a haber bloqueos y restricciones a medida que se propagaba el virus.

La escuela donde trabajaba cerró indefinidamente. Esperé durante cuatro meses mientras mis ahorros disminuían, pues pagaba el alquiler, los servicios básicos y otras cosas esenciales sin recibir ningún ingreso.

Luego China cerró las fronteras a los extranjeros para detener los casos importados, pero muchas personas tradujeron de manera errónea "importado" a "extranjero". La reacción de los chinos fue inimaginable. De repente los extranjeros eran vistos como la razón por la cual el virus se estaba propagando. La policía me detuvo varias veces a pesar de tener permisos legales, me negaron el acceso a alimentos, agua, medicinas y mascarillas, me impidieron usar el transporte público. Aparecieron avisos por todas partes, en los escaparates, cafeterías, restaurantes, que decían: "No se aceptan extranjeros".

Las personas que consideraba como amigos comenzaron a evitarme o me gritaban insultos como "Vuélvete a casa, virus extraño", cuando me veían pasar. Desde entonces, comenzaron los desalojos masivos. Los extranjeros eran desalojados sin previo aviso. Yo vivía con miedo de salir de mi apartamento en caso de que no me permitieran volver a entrar. El estrés y la ansiedad no tardaron en pasar factura: no podía dormir, no podía comer. Era hora de irse, y sonaba más fácil de decir que de hacer.

Pocos vuelos operaban en esos momentos y, como si eso no fuera poco, estaban cobrando muchísimo más de lo que costaba un boleto. Había dos vuelos que costaban 3000 euros cada uno, yo los reservé, pero fueron cancelados y el reembolso quedó pendiente. Después de tantos meses viviendo de mis ahorros, el costo de dos vuelos cancelados significaba que no podía correr el riesgo de comprar otro boleto, pues ya no tenía suficiente dinero. Afortunadamente, la amabilidad de los buenos amigos que tengo en el Reino Unido me ayudo a conseguir, con 10 horas de anticipación, un vuelo para salir de China y, además, me ofrecieron su casa para quedarme con ellos por el tiempo que fuese necesario.

No tuve tiempo de despedirme de nadie, vaciar mi departamento o incluso empacar lo que quería. Salí de China con toda una vida de buenos recuerdos eclipsados por la experiencia del racismo y dos maletas de "cosas esenciales".

Pero me niego a rendirme sin luchar. Estoy construyendo un negocio de enseñanza-aprendizaje en línea. También he estado aprendiendo español durante casi un año con una maestra de Venezuela. Las clases con ella me están ayudando a centrarme en un viaje a América del Sur. Esto me da la esperanza de tener un futuro en un mundo después del COVID, aunque será en un mundo diferente al que esperaba.

Sé que el mundo no se está terminando, simplemente está en pausa por un tiempo.

Christine's home language is English.

At Granda's funeral

Barbara Addison

Et wes ower canny thocht Jackie wytin for the procession tae appear on the big road abeen the hoose. Granny conwyed tae praivat as wes the wye, ben the hoose teemit, the weemin kwed clap dishes an maet doon for the murners return. There wes't! The men mairchen ahin the hearse in Sunday claes an Homburg hats. '**Holy Jimmy's procession**' sang the chaumer o her min. She wheepit roon.

Uncle Barry - the ither oolt o the faimily - sat. So, he hedna jined the men. Black hair and een socht the ower fair an blue een as afore. Winnerin, winnerin the same.

Fa'd bi ferst?

'Cam oot bi bus fae Aiberdeen?' he speirt. 'Ony bather?' Na. She hidna puked thes time.

The unaskit wes hingin atween them. Somebody hed tae mak a start.

'Aye. Ah cam yestreen,' she began. 'Granny Nellie's at Mam's hoose, ye ken...'

'Oh aye ah heard aboot it fae them baith. Andra an Betnay.'

She'd felt fit? Nae the forebodin o the toon. It wes his mither-in-law's bidin fan he hed fae that bathered hem: nae a sudden daith. Thon reed heid lauchin as they grat.

'Weel, Granny - Granny Nellie that es - jist said that 'yer puir Grandakie' got a recht shift.'

'That's Nellie speak,' reponed Barry. 'An she's recht, he continued.' Thi were sittin here jist sittin ye ken her en her cheer an hem in hes. Aa o a sudden hes legs thrashed aboot. A kina fit. She helpit hem throu tae thir bed in the back room, sed she'd tak hem a cuppa. Fan shi ded, he wes deid. That's fit she telt hes fan she cam roon fur the phone. Ye ken he widna lat a phone or onything en.

Jackie kent that muckle fae Granny hersel fae the necht afore. Granny sittin dignified in the new black frock brocht doon by her daughter-in-law. And Betnay saying it wes fine tho nae the ane maist suited tae her. Et wes ower dear.

But Uncle Ba wes speakin, 'Ded ye ken the doctor wantit a - fit dev ye caa't - an autopsy?'

'Naebody sed,' Jackie returned.

'Na. They widna. The aul leddie widna hae that. Nae recht an a thon. Ah mean et's nae Burke an Hare, es't.? Jist the law.'

'An?'

'That's fit wye the funeral's taen langer then fower days. The doc pit doon hairt failure on the certificate.'

Thur een held. Finally, Barry burst oot, 'Dev **ye** thenk the aul leddie did hem in?' Jackie braithed a breath. That'd been her an a, 'Na. Ah dinna thenk so. If she'd been guan tae dee that, she'dve deent lang ago.' And hated hersel.

Barry settled a thochtie. Baith wer disappintit.

Barbara's home language is Scots (Doric).

Limerick sobre un niño que amaba el español

Robbie Shelbourne

Era un niño que amaba el español
de sus vacaciones familiares en el sol.
Esta lengua era muy extraña,
con sus ritmos de muchas palabras.
El inglés no era suficiente
y soñó con un día charlar con esa gente,
así que se dijo a sí mismo que aprendería
por la nueva vida que él construiría.

Sin progreso, ingresó en la secundaria
donde el niño aprendió otra lengua.
¡Lamentablemente aprendió francés!
Es bonito pero no más de un mes,
porque podía sentir el español en sus venas
y la vida en inglés era como cadenas.
Sin castellano, persiguió otra carrera,
y como futbolista recibió una grata oferta:

Una oportunidad de jugar en Las Palmas
con una camiseta amarilla de esperanzas.
Pero su cuerpo se rompió con el fútbol,
y sus sueños cayeron como un árbol.
Buscó otra vez una manera

de aprender español, pero no estaba cerca.
Casi quince años pasarían,
y sin planes concretos las puertas se cerrarían.

Pero en su treinta cumpleaños, las cosas cambiaron.
En la Universidad Abierta una oportunidad le dieron:
Estudiando temas que le interesaban,
con profesores que le ayudaban,
se inscribió para Español e Historia,
con sueños nuevos para una vida nueva.
Ahora escribe este poema con palabras españolas
y a la Universidad Abierta quiere dar las gracias.

Robbie's home language is English.

A strange journey

Elizabeth Amri

It was summertime in Glasgow. It was Alice's favourite season. The days were warm and the evenings were long. The only drawback for her was her grass allergy.

This morning, her walk to the bus station was filled with glorious sunshine but her hay fever was playing up. Her eyes were red and swollen and her nose was tingling. Already her make-up was smudged and it was only 8.15 in the morning.

She arrived at the bus station as her bus was pulling up to the stop. She could feel the tingling in her nose ready to turn into a sneeze so she took out her hanky from her pocket and waited for the sneeze to come. 'Achoo!' Thank goodness she had her hanky at the ready.

She got on the bus. She handed the driver her fare and he handed her the ticket. 'Thank you' she said and he replied 'Merci.' 'Oh, a French-speaking bus driver,' she mused 'or maybe he's just practising a new language.' She did that herself when she tried to learn French a few years ago.

She walked along the aisle looking for a seat. About halfway up she spotted a space next to a middle-aged man but he had his bag sitting on the seat. She walked up and asked him if he could move his bag so she could sit and he spoke to her in what also appeared to be French although she couldn't be sure as he spoke so fast. She just gestured with a wave of her hand, which the man understood. « Ah – mon sac » he said, and removed his bag.

'That's strange,' she thought, 'another French speaker.'

She sat down and proceeded to look at the newspaper of the passenger in front of her. There was a photo of Donald Trump but the headline read « Donald Trump est à Londres, défendant un Brexit dur et son « ami » Boris Johnson. » 'Wait, what the hell is going on?' she thought, 'there must be a convention or something with all these French people on board.' She decided to just look out of the window instead. She usually found that quite soothing, and they would be approaching Glasgow city centre soon. She squealed suddenly 'No, this is not right. Is this a joke?' The direction sign outside her window stated *Paris centre ville 3km.*

Was she dreaming? Had she not woken this morning? She pinched herself. 'Ouch.' Yes, she was definitely awake. She was starting to hyperventilate, could feel a panic attack coming. 'I'll put my head between my knees' she thought and as she did this she sneezed again. 'Achoo.'

The man beside her was trying to get past. She looked up and he said, 'This is my stop, can I get by?' Then the driver announced, 'Next stop, Glasgow City Centre.' Both sounding very Glaswegian now.

'What a strange journey' she thought and alighted from the bus. Then she sneezed again.

A woman beside her extended a handkerchief and said 'Gesundheit.'

Elizabeth's home language is English.

我的不同世界 - Reflections during the coronavirus lockdown

Dr Diane Saxon

四月到达了，但是今年我没有如常去中国。四月在上海很漂亮。可是今年四月我在家，在英国。由于冠状病毒封锁，所以我不能去上海见我的家人。

我从没想过我会去中国，可是八年前左右我儿子和他的中国女朋友结婚了，所以现在我每年去中国两次。第一次去是因为我的亲家邀请我去参加婚礼宴会。婚宴是为她的家人，朋友和同事摆的。有约200人在那里。作为英国客人，我们很荣幸！有很多菜吃，有些我们不知道是什么，而且每个客人回家时都有一个红包，里面有一个礼物，一些糖果和香烟。我们很喜欢这个宴会。我们尝了新的食物并且见了我们的中国新朋友。

这八年中我看到了这个惊人的国家的一些方面。在北京，我参观了很多历史和文化遗址。我在长城上走了走。我体验了拥挤的人群和交通堵塞！我从北京去上海坐了高速列车。在苏州我看了很多美丽的花园。在西安我欣赏了兵马俑。我很喜欢中国菜，学会了用筷子。我参观了一些购物中心，而且去了湿市场买东西。

现在我们的家人住在上海，所以我们正在探索上海地区。上海有很多风光摩登建筑，一些极高大。这个城市是巨大和国际化的，但老上海往往只有几条街。这个城市有很多餐厅和各种各样的美食可供选择。我很喜欢饺子，我最喜欢是的小笼包。这是一个上海的名菜。

和别的城市比，上海有更多的人说英语，但是如果你不知道中文，读指路牌或者超市标签是很困难的。有时出租车司机不明白我们说什么或者我们想要去哪里！

所以我决定了我需要尝试学中文。我买了一些书，也上过一些课，而且我尝试了一些互联网应用程序，可是我发现学中文不容易。我工作的开放大学提供汉语课程，所以去年十月我开始学习他们的课程。我享受学习中文，尤其是能够与其他学生和老师在网上交谈。我喜欢了解不同国家的语言和文化，这是通向另一个世界的窗口！

　　我希望生活恢复常态，我能再去中国，可望年底前。现在开放大学的课程完了，可是当然我还有许多东西要学。我的学习将继续！

Diane's home language is English.

Bienvenu à vos destins

Heidi Gray

« Il y avait trois portes. »

The story always started the same. My grandmother would be sitting in her chair, staring into space, and I would take that as my cue to come and sit at her feet and listen.

« Trois portes pour sortir. La première a été détruite, à cause des personnes contaminées qui voulaient entrer. La deuxième a été bloquée à cause des personnes qui voulaient s'échapper, et la troisième est perdue, mais elle est toujours là. Quand elle est ouverte, le soleil va illuminer La Ruche, et on sera libre : notre destin. »

She would always smile at this point, probably imagining the moment the sunlight would warm her skin. When she was much older, she would repeat this story, like a mantra. Over and over again. These doors had been escape routes from the world. They closed off the danger but also the sunlight – nothing could get through.

What was behind the third door? My sister and I would spend nights imagining that lost world, the world above The Hive. The years slowly passed, and The Hive set us to work, and we soon forgot our childish fantasies.

* * *

Bienvenue à vos destins : bâtir un meilleur avenir

The slogan was all over The Hive. Endlessly advertised across the dark walls: dedicated workers, fulfilling their destiny. The women in the posters were muscled, with tools in their hands and a sheen of sweat shining across their faces, they were smiling too, their rosy cheeks glowing in the florescent light. I noticed the senate in the background standing on their podium, smiling graciously down, applauding the busy workers.

« Salut ma poulette, t'es dans la lune encore ? Dépêche-toi, sinon on va être en retard. »

She was right of course. If late, I would be accused of shirking my responsibility and everyone must play their part in The Hive, or else. This time they needed builders, to expand The Hive. Last time it had been farming. That was where my sister had made the ultimate Hive Sacrifice. Still, she had been doing it for The Hive, and there was no better way to go. « Ses efforts vont nourrir les générations à venir » they'd said at the funeral. Mother had cried with pride.

So it began. Day after day, my body slowly weakening under the strain. I lost count of how long I had been down there and how many tunnels we had dug, deeper and deeper, kilometre after kilometre. Reclaiming old tunnels, creating new ones. It was endless.

Endless: a meaningless word in The Hive. While excavating an old tunnel, we came across a green door, half buried in rubble. Written on it was *SORTIE DE SECOURS*. I knew straight away what it was, what it meant. My grandmother's voice echoed in my ears: « la troisième est perdue, mais elle est toujours là. »

« Bienvenue à vos destins. »

This was *my* destiny, to be free.

Heidi's home language is English.

Das Kulturkaleidoskop

Liam Flin

Vor einigen Jahren mussten Finn und Lena die Schule abbrechen, weil sie für das Familienhotel arbeiten mussten. In der Regel mussten sie Zeit mit Putzen und Kaffee kochen verbringen und in diesem Jahr wurden sie gezwungen, Papiere im Keller zu zerkleinern. Der Keller war sowohl verschmutzt als auch langweilig, aber alles würde sich dort bald verändern.

Sie sortierten die Papiere, aber Finn fühlte sich genervt und er rückte auf seinem Stuhle hin und her bis... krach! Lena lief schnell zu ihrem Bruder, der gefallen, aber nicht verletzt war. Er stürzte gegen eine Wandkarte und in ein unentdecktes Zimmer.

Die erstaunten Geschwister erforschten, was wie ein enger Flur erscheint, aber es enthielt zahlreiche Bilder. Es war eine versteckte Galerie. Die Kinder konnten nur einmal im Jahr ihre Freunde besuchen und deshalb würden sie immer die Gelegenheit ergreifen, Abenteuer zu erleben.

Die Bilder waren leuchtend und verlockend und sie konnten der Versuchung nicht mehr widerstehen, die Gemälde zu berühren. Jedoch kam in diesem Moment aus einem Bild ein Regenbogen und die Kinder verschwanden.

Jetzt fanden sie sich im Bild des Taj Mahals wieder, aber sie konnten sich immer noch bewegen und reden. Sie sonnten sich in dem nährenden Sonnenlicht Indiens und in dem strahlenden Leuchten des Monuments. Es war das Schlaraffenland. Dann saßen sie in der Nähe von einem Reflexionsbecken, aber das Wasser schlug hoch und zog die Kinder hinein.

Als sie auftauchten, waren sie nun in einer Wasserfontäne, die von einer Menge umgeben war. Die Menge tanzte und die Leute trugen Totenkopfmasken vor dem Hintergrund der bunten Bauten.

„Entschuldigung, wo sind wir?", fragte Finn.

„Hola amigo! Es el Día de Muertos!" antwortete schnell ein Mann.

Die Geschwister wurden von einem Feuerwerk am Himmel fasziniert, aber dann sahen sie herab und sie bemerkten, dass sie jetzt irgendwo anders waren. Es gab auch den Geruch von frischem Brot und jemand spielte das Akkordeon. Sie waren in Paris.

Der elegante Eiffelturm blickte über die Stadt und in diesem Moment fühlten sich Finn und Lena entspannt und herzlich. Aber plötzlich fuhr ein Radfahrer durch eine Pfütze und sie wurden mit kaltem Wasser benetzt. Das Wasser wurde kälter und stärker und der kalte Wind ließ sie erschauern.

Der isländische Wasserfall „Gullfoss" war vor ihnen und sein ohrenbetäubendes Donnern warf sie in ihren Keller zurück. Sie umarmten sich und dann sahen sie die Bilder, die sie umgaben. Es gab Bilder des Taj Mahals, des mexikanischen Einkaufszentrums, eines pariserischen Cafés und des Wasserfalls.

Aber gab es auch Bilder des Big Bens, des Amazonas und des Uluru. Sie wollten lebenslang Abenteuer erleben und jetzt fanden sie in ihrem eigenen Keller zahlreiche neue Welten. Sie fanden ihr eigenes Kulturkaleidoskop.

Liam's home language is English.

Breakfast whiskey

Ciarán Logue

"Cómo va, Fintan?" I had been used to communicating in broken Spanish on occasion with Raul, a madrileño. Now Raul's colleague, Sergio, a Peruvian, appeared and hit me with that while in full storytelling mode. "*Perdón, no te entiendo,*" I replied; a phrase I was used to deploying. The Jameson hangover didn't help. "How it go?!" Sergio suggested as a rough and obvious translation. The penny dropped. "Oh, of course! Sorry! Erm, *muy bien, ¿y tú?* One moment, *un momento,*" I said and ducked into the room to dig out a bottle of water. I winced back onto the balcony, shifting the old Celtic holdall I had arrived with; functional but battered and by no means classy. Raul's patchily-shaven head swivelled left and right on the neighbouring balcony at the same moment, his indignant eyebrows giving the look of a man who wanted better for himself. He turned to check his reflection and glanced across the plaza as he readied for the rest of my story.

Sergio, waiting patiently, gazed down to the street. "Mira, los micros circulan, a pesar del confinamiento."

"*Micros?*" I queried.

"City buses," clarified Raul.

I continued, "Anyway, she warns the living of an impending death... an arriving death, by knocking on your window or door." I tapped the table with my knuckles.

"When you open the door, there is no-one. *No hay nadie.* They say if you hear her cry you won't forget it.... a sound that will raise the hairs on the back of your neck."

I attempted to clarify my last sentence by pulling on my neck hairs and then downed what remained of a bottle of Estrella.

"That's the legend of the *bean sí*."

I scribbled the phonetically identical version, *Banshee*, on a post-it for them to research later.

I could keep the hotel bar going myself – under normal circumstances. That's what the others muttered. But this wasn't normal. The first two weeks of lockdown were enough for me to rid the bar of its meagre supplies. Hotel Santo Domingo was home for now, for the two lads and I - a summer job that had become long-term for us maintenance staff who had decided to remain there. At first the solitude was bliss; I was going to start that novel I had long intended to write. But the isolation was beginning to wear thin and the days dragged. Storytelling on the balconies had become a nightly ritual.

"That's my story. Anyway, what about Madrid?" I asked.

"There is La Casa de las Siete Chimeneas. A young woman was dead there with broke heart because she lost her man. She appear much time in house since her died centuries ago, sometime with torch." Raul's muddled English made his intro more engaging. "I prefer the story of *bean sí*," Sergio interrupted.

An insignificant river across the plaza, dark and stagnant, epitomised the summer ahead - long, forlorn, uneventful, yet forming a permanent mark on the landscape and those within it.

Ciarán's home language is English.

Le gardien du Dervallières F.C.

Eileanoir Blair

La première fois que je suis allée au Stade des Dervallières avec Felicity (également assistante d'anglais avec Erasmus et amatrice de foot), je dois avouer que j'éprouvais une certaine appréhension, car à mesure qu'on avançait à vélo, le paysage changeait radicalement. Les maisons élégantes étaient remplacées par d'énormes HLM, laides et vétustes. Cependant, mes craintes furent vite dissipées quand les joueurs, huit hommes et une femme de divers pays, nous accueillirent chaleureusement. Mieux encore, je marquai deux buts et entre Felicity et moi, nous leur montrâmes que les femmes ont toute leur place sur le terrain !

Le lendemain, dans la cantine des profs, nous racontâmes à nos collègues notre aventure aux Dervallières. Ils échangèrent des regards inquiets. « C'est trop dangereux, le quartier est miné par le trafic de drogue ! », le prof de physique s'exclama. Effectivement, c'était inquiétant mais je n'allais certainement pas renoncer à mon activité préférée.

Un soir, après plusieurs semaines d'extase, un personnage déplaisant, qui nous regardait, me faisait constamment des remarques inappropriées. Je n'arrivais pas à me concentrer et je jouai atrocement. Après, je racontai tout à Felicity et à Aziz, le gardien de notre équipe. Ce dernier était choqué et voulait le confronter. Je dus attraper son bras pour le retenir, ne voulant pas une bagarre ! En effet, depuis notre première rencontre, je m'entendais très bien avec ce grand homme d'origine algérienne, avec les yeux marron et les cheveux bouclés. Pourtant, quand il voulut me protéger, je commençai à le voir sous un nouveau jour.

Le jour suivant je vis un article intitulé « Coups de feu mortels aux Dervallières ». Pour Felicity, c'était le comble, elle refusa de retourner au foot. Moi, j'étais effrayée d'y aller toute seule mais je savais que quand j'y serais, Aziz me protégerait. Après le match Aziz, qui voyait que j'avais peur, offrit de m'accompagner sur le chemin de retour, bien qu'il habite juste à côté du stade. J'acceptai avec reconnaissance et avec lui, le voyage de retour fut presque meilleur que le match !

Les mois passèrent très vite et chaque jeudi soir après avoir joué au foot, Aziz m'accompagnait à l'internat. Naturellement, nos coéquipiers commençaient à faire des remarques sur nos randonnées à vélo nocturnes. Cela nous gênait parce qu'il était musulman et moi chrétienne donc nous savions que, malgré l'attirance mutuelle, nous ne pourrions jamais être ensemble ; nos valeurs fondamentales étaient incompatibles.

« A la prochaine fois » Aziz a crié au portail de mon école après le match du 12 mars. Ensuite, la même nuit, j'ai appris que les pays européens avaient commencé à fermer leurs frontières à cause du Covid-19. Pour ne pas être coincée en France, j'ai dû rentrer en Irlande immédiatement donc j'ai pris le premier vol disponible, le cœur lourd, sans avoir dit adieu à Aziz. Je ne sais pas combien de temps le confinement durera ni si je vais pouvoir revenir à Nantes. Tout ce que je sais c'est qu'une partie de moi est restée sur le terrain du F.C. Dervallières.

Eileanoir's home language is English.

Worlds apart

Zoe Hickton

Peeping over the banisters at the top of the stairs, my senses were overwhelmed by sights and smells that my five-year-old brain couldn't process. A strange smell was wafting up from the sitting room: like the 'Zip' firelighters Dad used when the stove went out and he couldn't get it going again. Firelighters were dangerous. Dad had said so.

'No Marty, don't put that in yer gob, you'll be shittin' through the eye of a needle for a week!'

The sitting room door was ajar. I could see Dad, but I knew there were other people there too from the voices. My mum definitely, and a few others by the sound of it. I could hear Mum now…

'We need something fresh, Jerry. There's no other way of generating revenue and if things don't pick up soon, we're sunk!'

There was a murmur of agreement: it sounded menacing, like the low hum from a wasps' nest. I craned my neck. Dad was standing near the door now with some sort of big knife in his hand! Another danger! A remembered warning came into my mind:

'No Marty, that'll cut yer bloody fingers off soon as it'll look at ya! Give it 'ere lad!'

What was going on? As I watched, horrified, he brought the shiny blade up to his face, tipped his head far back and started to put it in his mouth! The unseen wasp-people in the room did nothing to stop him! I felt cold all over, then strangely warm as my five-year-old bladder gave way.

'No Daddy, no!'

I tumbled down the stairs exploding into the room and crashing into my Dad, who retched and collapsed onto the storm-at-sea blues of the carpet. The knife shot out of his gaping mouth, landing at mother's feet. She leapt up, torn between comforting her stricken son and checking for signs of life in her prostrate husband. The silence was broken by Dad. Crawling to his knees, he rasped out possibly his last words....

'Bloody hell, Marty, we've told ya before not to bother us when we're practicing. Ya could 'ave pinging well done for me kiddo!'

As the shock receded and the familiar room came into focus, I gazed around, at the shocked faces of my parents and their circus troop: fire eater Dan (that explained the whiff of 'Eau de Zip': there were paraffin stains on his red shirt), Tony, the lugubrious clown, sadder than ever as the chaos unfolded round him, and of course my dad, ring master and now, apparently, sword swallower. With a shudder I realised that there was also me: Marty 'the Missile', destined, in my parents' minds, to be the greatest human canon ball the world had ever seen.

I wept then, with despair for my future. How could I tell them that there burned inside me a passion for a different world? A world of numbers that I knew would only be satisfied by a job in accountancy.

Zoe's home language is English.

· Day two ·

Are the stars more beautiful at Qinghai lake? 青海湖的星星更美吗?

Ruaridh Maclean

　　那天有人问我在青海湖是否能看到闪烁而又美丽的星星，我即刻想起我在青海湖的时候……

　　去年暑假，我坐上了从新疆开往西宁的火车。一路上，天气炎热也干燥得厉害，所以我一直是短裤和T恤在身。到了西宁以后，我把我的行李扔在了宾馆，小憩了一会儿，然后只带了一点装备坐上了去青海湖的大巴。青海湖的小镇的天气还好，不冷也不热。后来，我找到了一家很小的旅店，他们的房间都是在外面，像活动房屋一样。我把东西留在了这个小旅店里，租了辆自行车，然后向青海湖骑去。

　　我沿着小路骑行，一边是无边无际的青海湖，另一边则是深绿色的高草原，头顶的云很低，淡淡的有着不可思议的色彩。天气有些冷，但我觉得骑得快点就感受不到了。湖岸有几只牦牛，我停了一会儿，拍了些许照片，看看牦牛，感受这里的一切。

　　后来，天气越来越冷，一丝丝凉意伴随着一滴滴雨水向我袭来。可怜的我当时还穿着短裤和T恤，也没有带其他的衣服。我快速骑上了自行车，沿着小路疯狂地骑行。很快雨越下越大，然后变成了倾盆而下的暴雨，温度越来越低，手冷得厉害，我活生生变成了一只落汤鸡。

　　忽然间，我看到了几个民族帐篷，第一个帐篷里有一个妇女和一只狗，妇女似乎在准备晚上的饭菜。她一看到我落汤鸡般的样子就请我进屋蹲在炉边烤火。我在炉边冻得瑟瑟发抖，突然间，一道闪电从天空中劈了下来，击中了离帐篷很近的地方，紧接着就是一声可怕的巨雷。

　　帐篷里的妇女吓得叫了起来，狗也跟着汪汪地叫。尽管我自己不怕雷，我也被吓得跳了起来。吓死我了！就这样，我在那间帐篷里等了几个小时，一边发抖，一边看着外面荒凉的风景。

后来来了一辆卡车，好心的司机师傅把我带回了小旅店。天已经变黑了，一片乌黑。又冷又累生无可恋的我终于回到房间。更可怜的是旅店的房间没有热水，也没有空调，被子也特别的薄，无奈的我爬上了床，然后缩成一团。心想，我怎么就没看天气预报呢！

青海湖的星星，一颗也没看到。

现在想想那时候的故事，我觉得我也算是个笨蛋的歪果仁。我还希望有一天能再回去青海湖看一看。

Ruaridh's home language is English.

Das Dingsbums

Judith Jaquet

Startled early from sleep by the piercing whistle of a red kite, I decide to be the proverbial early bird and catch the worm.

The 2-metre queues outside the shops in my local high street will be practically non-existent at this hour… There will still be croissants and cinnamon rolls in the bakery, hand sanitiser and toilet rolls in the pharmacy and dishwasher tablets in the supermarket!

Full of optimism, I head out.

Sure enough, the spaces between the neon yellow 2-metre markers laddering the pavement outside the bakery are empty. No need to queue! Oh good, they're open…

'Guten Tag! Wie kann ich Ihnen helfen?'

'Excuse me?'

'Was kann ich für Sie tun?'

I imagine my face is a picture. Really? Croissants in *German*? Cinnamon rolls? Just stick to bread rolls…

'Entschuldigung… vier Brötchen bitte.' (I feel that I'm in a year 7 German class although obviously, currently, it would be via zoom.)

'Sonst noch etwas?'

'Langsamer bitte!'

'Möchten… Sie… sonst… noch… etwas?'

'Nein danke, das ist alles.' (Unfortunately.)

I swiftly settle the bill. Thank goodness I didn't have to struggle with any dative or accusative constructions at this hour of the day, not to mention genitive declensions...

Bread rolls in hand, I happily discover entirely vacant zones beside the pharmacy. Just toilet rolls and hand gel... and some hydrocortisone cream for eczema.

'Bonjour, madame. Je peux vous aider?'

The assistant does have a lovely smile, but that's the hydrocortisone cream out the window.

'Vous pouvez répéter, s'il vous plaît?' (Such a useful question. It's the subsequent reply that's usually the problem.)

'Bien sûr, madame. Est-ce que je peux vous aider?'

(Sadly, no.) Bizarrely, das Klopapier pops into my head, but that won't help me now. Certainly not with the hydrocortisone cream. I really want to say 'das Dingsbums' as it's such a super word.

'Oui, madame, une brosse à dents, s'il vous plaît!' (A toothbrush? Really?! Actually, spare toothbrushes *are* always handy for those unexpected guests, though naturally not just now.)

I head for the supermarket.

Wonderful. No socially distanced queue here either. I obediently follow the yellow arrows around the store and grab the dishwasher tablets (this must be the time of day to find them in stock!). I then have to do another lap of the shop, as I remember I can buy my hand sanitiser and toilet rolls here too. It's rather like a board game of snakes & ladders.

No queue at the till either.

A really smiley girl!

'¡Hola! ¡Buenos días!'

(Heck.)

'¡Hola!' (Bother, I *never* remember the 'h' is silent.)

'¿Algo más?' She's still smiling.

'¿Perdón? ¿Me lo puede repetir?' (Luckily, I'd spent quite a bit of time on the 'asking for repetition' section in my Spanish course.)

'¿Otra cosita?'

'La cuenta, por favor.' (Oops, that's for restaurants.)

She's really smiling now.

'¿Cuánto es?' (Thank goodness I've remembered the right question word. There really are just too many.)

'Mum?!'

My smiling daughter. No bill to pay. Just the best lockdown breakfast in bed.

Judith's home language is English.

Ma vie en Angleterre après m'être enfui de chez moi...

Paul B Naylor

Bonjour à tous, c'est merveilleux de votre part de m'accueillir avec cette fête de nouveau à Saint-Valery-sur-Somme, ici en Picardie, après tant d'années d'absence. Si vous êtes assez âgés, vous vous souvenez peut-être que je m'appelle François Cloutier. Je me suis enfui à l'âge de 15 ans en 1643 pour m'engager dans la marine en combattant les Anglais. Malheureusement, peu de temps après, j'ai été capturé et emmené travailler dans une ferme à Eyam, un village du Derbyshire. Cependant, une fois que j'ai appris un peu d'anglais, la vie y était bonne car j'ai rencontré et suis tombé amoureux de Mary, une femme du coin. Nous nous sommes mariés en 1652 et avons eu deux enfants. Mais la vie à Eyam a changé radicalement en juin 1665.

Robert Hill, un tailleur local, tomba bientôt malade après avoir déballé du tissu de Londres et il mourut huit jours plus tard. Londres était un centre important de peste noire en Europe à l'époque et nous pensons que des puces porteuses de la peste, cachées dans le tissu, ont infecté Robert. Un peu plus tard, bien qu'elle n'ait elle-même jamais été infectée, Mabel Brown a dû traîner les corps de six de ses enfants et de son mari hors de leur maison et les enterrer dans un champ voisin, le tout en l'espace de huit jours. Les habitants d'un village voisin se tenaient sur une colline et regardaient Mabel, trop effrayés pour l'aider. De nombreux autres villageois sont tombés malades et sont morts, dont la femme de

George Prudhomme, le recteur d'Eyam, et très tristement pour moi, ma femme et mes deux enfants. John Mason a également perdu sa femme et son fils mais, comme il l'a dit, « je n'ai pas peur. J'ai eu la peste, donc je ne l'aurai plus », et il est devenu l'enterreur des morts d'Eyam principalement parce que, comme l'a dit un villageois, « cela signifiait qu'il pouvait prendre les affaires des victimes ! »

Entre septembre et décembre 1665, 42 des 700 villageois sont morts. Les survivants ont désespérément voulu quitter le village. Cependant, Prudhomme pensait que quitter le village porterait la maladie dans les villes voisines comme Sheffield. Il avait également entendu parler du succès de la mise en quarantaine des personnes pendant l'épidémie de peste noire du 14ème siècle à Florence et pensait que cela pourrait fonctionner à Eyam. Il a donc organisé une réunion en plein air pour éviter de propager l'infection afin d'essayer de persuader les villageois qu'un cordon sanitaire était nécessaire, de manière désintéressée, pour protéger les autres. Bien que de nombreux villageois aient été réticents, tous ont fini par accepter l'idée et la quarantaine a commencé immédiatement. Le 1er novembre, le virus avait disparu, mais les trois quarts des villageois aussi !

Mary et mes enfants n'étant plus, je me suis senti très seul à Eyam, alors je suis revenu ici pour être avec vous tous. Prions pour que cette terrible peste ne nous rende jamais visite. Maintenant, continuons avec le fromage et le vin, et bonne santé!

Paul's home language is English.

Verónica

Huw Jones

Gareth estaba feliz. Después de años de estudiar español, había decidido que para hablar como un nativo debía vivir como los españoles, y ahora viajaba por el país en su gran coche amarillo con su amiga, Verónica. La verdad es que tenía que ser un coche de tamaño familiar porque Verónica era una señora bastante grande. Eran una pareja extraña, pero la relación era perfecta, y cuando la gente los veía juntos, siempre se acercaba a hablar con ellos.

Pero ¿cómo se conocieron? Bueno, unos meses antes, Gareth se fue a vivir a un pueblo de Extremadura para acostumbrarse a escuchar la lengua y entender las tradiciones. Pero había una costumbre muy extraña, y cuando Gareth se enteró de ella, quedó confundido y francamente preocupado. Habló con sus nuevos amigos, que coincidieron en que en España era una práctica normal para cualquier largo viaje. Él pensó para sí mismo «Si todos los españoles lo hacen, entonces debe ser aceptable», pero se sentía mal.

Al final, fue a ver al sacerdote. Gareth le preguntó si esta tradición era normal. El sacerdote respondió:

—¡Claro que sí! Debes darte cuenta de que estás en un país diferente, así que haz lo que hacemos y te hará la vida más fácil.

Y con las palabras del sacerdote aún en su mente, Gareth preguntó a su vecino, el Sr. Calderón, si podía ayudarle. María, una de las hijas del Sr. Calderón, era morena e inteligente, y Gareth estaba enamorado de ella, pero al día siguiente el Sr. Calderón le dijo que Verónica lo acompañaría en su viaje. Echaría de menos a María, pero Verónica era tranquila y satisfaría sus necesidades.

Así que se fueron, viajando por todas partes, desde las playas de Huelva a las montañas de Cantabria, pero el recuerdo favorito de Gareth fue La Fiesta de San Fermín en Pamplona donde huyó de los toros mientras Verónica los perseguía. Un día, un anciano se acercó a ellos y le preguntó:

—¿Por qué tienes una vaca en tu coche?

Gareth respondió:

—¿Verónica? Es una tradición española.

El hombre dijo que no había oído hablar de esta costumbre y debía ser una tradición rara de Extremadura. Con el tiempo, Gareth se dio cuenta de que nadie en el resto de España lo sabía.

Unos meses más tarde, cuando Gareth y Verónica volvieron al pueblo, Gareth encontró al sacerdote y le dijo que la tradición de viajar con una vaca en el coche no era muy común. El sacerdote lo miró durante unos segundos, negó con la cabeza y dijo asombrado:

—¡Dios mío, estás loco! No necesitas una vaca para viajar, pero una baca para tu equipaje sería muy útil.

Gareth se rió:

—¡No es de extrañar que no tuviera espacio para mis maletas!

Gareth y María fueron felices juntos, y Verónica siguió soñando con San Fermín.

Huw's home language is Welsh.

When history meets Grandma

Eliza Curtain

The sunshine streamed radiantly into the worn living room. Six small glasses, three plastic beakers, and two sippy cups were dotted around the room. There were also three plates of thickly sliced banana bread, two jugs of juice, and one cup of tea. Grandma began.

'It originated when the man with the golden hair…'

'Grandma?' A child, no older than seven, interrupted. 'Are you talking about the President?'

A cry sounded from a girl about the same age, 'You absolute Covidiot, that's the man with the golden tan. Isn't it, Grandma?' Her cheeks flushed while she spoke.

The audience sighed as this was only the start of what would be another lengthy edition of the tale.

'Does he *really* shine like the sun?' queried another boy, who sat on his Grandma's lap, sippy cup in hand. She squeezed him tightly as she looked up at the ceiling.

'No, he doesn't. It all began many moons ago. The man with the golden hair imposed a lockdown on the townspeople…'

Small gasps erupted from the crowd of eleven children, all eager to hear the tale they've heard every year since they were born. A time-honoured family tradition. Their eyes gleamed with intrigue and horror at the events that were about to unfold from the small lady who sat innocently in her armchair.

'The people were locked in their homes, forced to wash their hands until their skin peeled off, subjected to constant quizzing over their general knowledge and would be ridiculed if they came last...'

'Grandma?'

'Yes, dear?'

'Can you remember the zombies this time? You know? The ones that don't know how to distance themselves in shops? You forgot last time and that's the best part,' said a girl squished in the corner of the sofa.

'Not for me. Too scary,' the boy trailed off as he was hushed with a glare from his sister.

A round face piped up 'We're not even close to the zombies yet. We still have the battle of W.F.H. When the children revolted against the adults,' squinting in the sun as she spoke.

'That's my favourite part. Tell that bit. Please. Pleaseeeeeee' pleaded another.

A spray of cake crumbs hailed onto the carpet. 'When's the battle of "No-more-loo" that Granddad told us last time? When all the toilet roll disappeared for no reason' His chubby fingers picked up the larger crumbs and shoved them into his already full mouth.

'I'll tell you everything if you all hush. Now, will you let me finish?'

A chorus of 'yeses' followed as they regathered to listen to the tale from a time long since forgotten. Grandma didn't have the heart to tell them it was only a few decades since it all *really* happened.

But the truth is always more interesting when history meets Grandma.

Eliza's home language is English.

A journey by train

Susan Cooper

Once upon a time, that is the way in which all English fairy tales begin.

Once upon a time, a group of people were travelling together in a train through Europe. They could have been typically English people minding their own business: reading a book, doing a crossword, looking out of the window, sleeping, praying, all thinking their own thoughts and taking very little notice of their fellow passengers.

Suddenly the train juddered to a halt.

Oh dear, said the English woman, what has happened?

Oh je, was ist passiert? sagte der Deutsche.

Oh mon Dieu, que s'est-il passé? dit la femme française.

Ay Dios mío, ¿qué ha pasado? dijo el español.

Oh cielo, cosa è successo? disse il prete italiano.

They all stare at each other. Niemand versteht, was der andere sagt. La française avait l'air anxieuse. El español cierra su libro. L'italiano guarda l'orologio.

To break the silence, pointing to herself, the English woman said hello, my name is Cynthia, and gesturing into the distance, I am travelling to Rome to study history and art.

Ebenso sagt der Deutsche, Guten Tag, mein Name ist Jörgen. Ich fahre nach Berlin zur Arbeit.

Bonjour, je m'appelle Françoise. Je voyage à Lyon pour rendre visite à mon amant.

Hola, me llamo Manuel, regreso con mi familia de Barcelona.

Ciao, sono Padre Giovanni, vado a Milano dove dirò messa in Cattedrale.

Ils commencent à se détendre. Wer wird was als nächstes verraten?

Cynthia dit, Je suis professeure en congé sabbatique.

Jörgen says, I am an actuary working for a large insurance company. I am divorced.

Dice Françoise, indicando la sua fede nuziale, sono sposata. Mio marito non sa del mio amante.

Manuel sagt, ich habe eine Frau und drei Kinder und ich bin Philosoph.

El padre Giovanni señala su collar y dice: No estoy casado, soy célibe.

Cynthia sospirò, una volta ho avuto una relazione...

Jörgen avoue avoir visité des bars et des prostituées.

Françoise gibt zu, dass sie das Geld ihres Mannes mag, bevorzugt aber die Gesellschaft ihres Geliebten.

Manuel ha avuto una relazione con il suo segretario.

Pater Giovanni träumt von dem jungen Mann, der die Briefe liefert.

Slowly the train begins to move, it gradually gathers pace. The occupants of the carriage look at each other in an embarrassed manner.

Cynthia returns to looking out the window, Jörgen kehrt zu seinem Kreuzworträtsel zurück, Françoise se rendort et rêve de son amant, Manuel abre su libro e padre Giovanni ricomincia a pregare.

And when the train stops and they leave the train, they do not even say goodbye to one another.

Susan's home language is English.

Le garçon dont les cheveux poussaient

Keith Brown

Léo allait chez le coiffeur lorsque sa mère a reçu un texto. Ce message marque le début du confinement contre une nouvelle épidémie. Léo ne pouvait plus se faire couper ses cheveux roux donc ils sont rentrés. Il était triste.

Les cheveux de Léo poussaient de plus en plus. Ces cheveux l'irritaient. Sa mère lui a fait un chignon, Léo était agacé et il est allé se coucher. Il s'est réveillé au bord d'un court de tennis. À sa plus grande surprise, il était sur le point de jouer contre le champion du monde. Léo a ramassé sa raquette et a joué pendant cinq heures jusqu'au moment où il a gagné le match. Maintenant, il était le champion du monde. Léo sautait de joie quand il s'est cogné la tête et s'est réveillé dans son lit.

Six semaines plus tard, les longs cheveux roux bouclés de Léo brillaient au soleil. Son frère Frédéric lui a demandé : « Quel est ton animal préféré ? ». Léo a répondu qu'il adorait les félins et s'est roulé en boule. Il se sentait un peu bizarre et a remarqué qu'il était assis dans une plaine. Il a baissé les yeux pour voir qu'il était un lion ! Son grand-père, qui avait faim, était malade et exposé au soleil. Il avait besoin d'aide. Léo a partagé sa nourriture et est parti chercher des médicaments dans la jungle voisine. C'est là qu'il a rencontré un éléphant sage. Il a parlé à l'éléphant de son grand-père, qui lui a conseillé de récolter les feuilles de Gotu Kola. Léo a remercié l'éléphant et a aussi cueilli une grande feuille pour lui faire de l'ombre. Quand Léo a levé les yeux, il a vu une grosse noix se précipiter vers sa tête. Il s'est réveillé à côté de son frère qui rugissait comme un lion.

Quelques mois plus tard, Léo maintenant a les cheveux très longs. Il attend ses grands-parents. Il est assis depuis longtemps et s'est endormi. Léo fait une sieste, puis se réveille à bord d'un petit navire. Il sentait la brise marine dans ses longs cheveux. L'aventurier Léo et son équipage allaient découvrir une nouvelle terre. À leur arrivée, ils découvrent qu'ils ne sont pas les premiers. Il y avait aussi une épidémie et donc Léo et ses aventuriers ont été mis en quarantaine. Léo a appris que les habitants de l'île testaient un vaccin et il a offert son aide. Toutefois, Léo avait peur des aiguilles et il s'est évanoui.

Son grand-père, Georges, lui demande s'il a bien dormi. Léo lui dit qu'il ne sait pas si le vaccin a marché. Un peu confus, George dit à Léo de mettre ses chaussures parce qu'ils vont chez le coiffeur. Léo se met à pleurer. Léo est maintenant triste que ses aventures aient peut-être pris fin.

Keith's home language is English.

A quarantine story

Anabel Prieto

I get up every day at a different time, usually early, because in Scotland the sun rises remarkably early. A strict routine is proving difficult and every day is different to the previous one.

Just before 6 am the trains start to pass. I live by a train station, so I hear the trains coming and going. At first the frequency is low, but then it slowly and steadily increases until it reaches every 5 minutes, just after 7 am. I could use this as an alarm clock, but it actually works as a lullaby for me. I really like trains and the rhythmic rattle soothes me.

Even if I wake up early, I like to stay in bed for a good while, listening to the noises of the neighbours: somebody's steps walking and making their wooden floor – my ceiling – crackle, water running down the pipes or someone flushing a distant toilet, doors opening and closing, the rolling of the wheels of the bins being taken out by the downstairs neighbour if it's a Wednesday... I never noticed all these sounds before and now I find them reassuring, even interesting.

Eventually I get up, get a coffee, and go back to bed, to read the news or whichever book I am with that day. After an hour or so, I truly get up and I do some yoga before having breakfast and starting the day of work or study.

I don't have a normal job anymore, but sometimes I get sent translations to do. It varies each week, but I've decided not to worry too much about money, since it's something that I can't do much about at the moment. I often end up studying one of the languages I am learning. When I feel too lazy to study or the weather out there is too tempting to stay inside, I go for a walk and explore the neighbourhood. I have been living in this flat nearly two years and I only discovered recently that I live near two beautiful parks and the river which I love.

My afternoons are usually spent in front of the screen, for some online course I am taking or to talk with friends and family. These hours are usually very rewarding, but afterwards I find myself exhausted and stay away from the screen for what's left of the day.

I usually end my day the same way I started it: in bed, with a hot drink and a book. Now and then I write, and if I am very lucky, it may be something good. But I also take it easy with that. I have learnt that sometimes there is no point in putting so much pressure on yourself and wanting to plan and control things. There are some things one cannot control. And that is OK, at least for now…

Anabel's home language is Spanish.

Die drei Philanthropinnen

Bubune K Sewornu

Drei Bäuerinnen lebten im Jahr 1980 auf der japanischen Insel Okinawa. Sie hiessen Xìnxīn, Yosa und Smile. In Okinawa haben sie einen kleinen Bauernhof der Hydrokultur gehabt und haben daran zusammen gearbeitet. Smile war Amerikanerin, Xìnxīn ist aus China gekommen und Yosa war Japanerin. Joy und Neisei waren die Kinder von Smile und Yosa. Xìnxīn hatte kein Kind und war die älteste Frau. Die achtjährigen Mädchen haben die örtliche Schule besucht und spielten gerne zusammen, wenn ihre Eltern und Xìnxīn beschlossen, ein Picknick am Strand zu machen oder im Park spazieren zu gehen.

Die fleissigen Frauen haben ihr Gemüse an die Menschen in Okinawa verkauft. Sie haben Fisch, Fleisch und andere landwirtschaftliche Produkte von ihrem lokalen Markt gekauft. Als ihre Kinder zwölf Jahre alt waren, hat Okinawa eine schwere Dürre erlebt. Es hat wenig Regen gegeben, und andere Landwirte, die auf den Boden angewiesen waren, konnten kein Getreide anbauen. Folglich gab es auf der Insel Okinawa Hungersnot. Die Leute in Okinawa haben nach Nahrung gesucht, um ihre Familien, Haustiere und Vieh zu füttern.

Deshalb trafen sich Yosa, Smile und Xìnxīn mit den Kindern im Park, um zu besprechen, wie sie den Menschen in Okinawa helfen könnten. Sie haben ein paar Imbisse und Getränke zum Teilen mitgebracht. Gleich an Anfang hat Xìnxīn Joy ein paar Kekse

gegeben, „非 常 感 谢 您", sagte Joy. Die drei Frauen und Joy
sprachen fliessend Englisch, während Neisei weniger Englisch
sprechen konnte. Smile lernt Japanisch ungern. Jetzt versuchte sie
Neisei ein paar Erdbeeren zu geben. Als sie dabei ist, ihr das Obst
zu geben, sagte Neisei, „I like, いただきます". Plötzlich hat sie den
Teller und die Erdbeeren auf den Boden fallengelassen. Auf
Japanisch heisst „itadakimasu", *ich bekomme es und werde es essen.* So
sagen immer die Japaner, bevor sie irgendetwas knabbern. Aus
Unwissenheit hat Smile gedacht, dass sie *„eat a duck and mouse"*
gehört hat. Deshalb ist sie in Verlegenheit geraten und hat
versprochen, Japanisch und Mandarin zu lernen.

Die Frauen haben sich entschieden, die Produktion auf ihrem
Bauernhof der Hydrokultur zu steigern. Ihr System der
Hydrokultur erntete Regenwasser und hat es im Überfluss gehabt.
Deshalb hatte die Dürre keinen Einfluss auf ihre Anbaumethode. Sie
zirkulierten und verwendeten das Regenwasser wieder. Dann wird
daher weniger Wasser benötigt. Die Pflanzen wachsen sehr schnell,
weil sie immer Nährstoff erhalten. Es gibt die Leuchtanzeige, die
Temperaturregelung und das automatisierte vertikale Stapelsystem
von Gestellen. Sie verwendeten auch kein Pestizid auf dem
Bauernhof. Es war eine fortschrittliche und vorteilhafte Methode
des Bauernhofs in der damaligen Zeit.

Sie hatten für sich genug Gemüse und Erdbeeren vom
Bauernhof. Dann haben sie auch frische Produkte an die Leute in
Okinawa verteilt. Sie haben den Alten und den kranken Leuten
geholfen. Die Gutherzigkeit, Zufriedenheit und Stütze unter den
Bürgern der Stadt halfen ihnen, die Dürre bis zum folgenden Jahr zu
überleben, als es reichlich geregnet hat und das Leben wieder
normal wurde. Danach lebten sie alle glücklich.

Bubune's home language is English.

Trasloco

Ashley Hall

Era un bell'appartamento. At the time! Bilocale. Soppalco. Well kind of. Terrazzino. Pizzofalcone. Bella zona. Pretty much as I had imagined. Vicino al centro ma anche al mare. It had my name on it. Le sedie Robin Dei. The oversized, salvaged 1970's industrial light bulb. Il palloncino di Bilumen. El aguacate. Frida and Matisse. She made it a home. It was never right without her there.

But you know, it was like the comfort of staying put was more painful than the temporary inconvenience of having to move. You get attached to things, but five was the limit. Diría que era la décima vez que lo hacía, pero, en realidad, era la primera de muchas con tu madre. Pushed by a feeling of an otherwise missed opportunity. Pulled by love or the allure of pride. That feeling you get from achieving something new and finding joy on the other side. Supongo que había fuerzas internas y externas. It was undeniable.

She was ready a year earlier. Ahora, su amiga dejaba su casa, así que había un lugar en el pueblo disponible para nosotros. Temporarily at least. Nothing like this, but it was perfect for us. You get signs. Hints. Por ejemplo: una colega estaba buscando casa también. La nuestra era la solución ideal. Tampoco tenía tanta seguridad de tener un trabajo allí después del verano. Sometimes you even get flashing neon signs with arrows. Pasar más tiempo separados no era una opción. Rimanere al quinto piano dietro la cupola neanche.

Miss each other? ¿Te acuerdas de las videollamadas? Eso hicimos cada día. Difficult? Yeah! Era muy duro. Besando pantallas. But in some kinda way it confirmed a lot.

Cuatro meses of solid isolation with afrobeats as the soundtrack. We'd done distance before. But it had gotten way too much. It was a couple of years before you came. Time there was officially up. It wasn't our future. It wasn't yours. I extracted all the juice that I could. Una lingua. Amici. Lavoro. Cultura. Formazione. We both did.

Además, llevaba cuatro meses trabajando en línea. It wasn't optional anymore. Confirmation that I had to jump again. She had already.

Then the parliament called. She deserved it.

Sapevo che bonjour and s'il vous plaît era lo siguiente.

How can you stay where you are and go where you're going?

Ashley's home language is English.

Bun numéro un

JB

Je suis assise dans le salon et je veux vous présenter notre lapin.
'No Bun! No! No Bun! Mum he's chewing your OU books, are they important?'

'Are they the ones on the floor? No, that's fine he can chew those.'

J'étudie à l'Open University depuis près de vingt ans et, en conséquence, j'ai accumulé un tas de livres de l'OU, dont la plupart n'ont pas été ouverts depuis longtemps. Ma fille vient juste de me dire : *'at least someone is using them now!'*

Je m'égare, le lapin est mignon. Il est né cette année, le 5 février, il est noir et blanc et il est arrivé chez nous le 31 mars. Ma fille, qui est revenue ici au début mars, m'a convaincue d'acheter un lapin. Décision prise, ma fille a commencé ses recherches. Il n'y avait que deux exigences – un lapin amical et la livraison à domicile selon les règles de distanciation sociale.

Le 31 mars, vers midi, la sonnette sonna. Ma fille travaillait (télé-travail), alors c'est moi qui ai ouvert la porte. Il n'y avait personne, mais il y avait une boîte sur le pas de la porte. J'ai soigneusement ramassé la boîte, et l'ai posée, doucement, sur le plancher dans le vestibule. Sans faire de bruit, j'ai ouvert, très lentement, la boîte. *He was so cute and so tiny and so scared!*

Bun was home :) Il vit avec nous depuis neuf semaines maintenant. On l'adore et il est totalement *spoilt!*

Il y a quelques semaines.....

'Mum, can we get another bun?'

'Sorry, what did you say?'

J'ai bien entendu ce qu'elle m'a demandé, mais je dois réfléchir un moment.

'He needs a friend, some company.'

'But we play with him and spend time with him and keep him company.'

'I know, but wouldn't it be nice if he had another bun to play with.'

'Yes, however, there are other things to consider.'

Bun nous a déjà coûté cher. Parmi les frais, il y avait un nouveau téléphone, un nouveau câble d'imprimante et une nouvelle lampe. J'imagine la vie avec encore un *bun*. *How could we keep watch over two active nibbling bunnies?* Malheureusement j'ai décidé que *bun* numéro deux *would have to wait.*

On adore *Bun*, et on espère qu'il nous adore. *He's fully settled here now, that's for sure.* Je répète, il est complètement à l'aise chez nous - il vit dans le salon, il mange dans le salon, il fait beaucoup de sauts de lapin dans le salon. En effet, c'est devenu son salon!

'Hello Bun, have you come to see what I'm doing? I'm writing about you :)'

Parfois je me demande si *Bun* restera ici lorsque ma fille déménagera. Cela sera peut-être le moment pour *bun* numéro deux, mon *bun* :)

BTW, I've already chosen a name for bun numéro deux - Chignon :)

JB's home language is English.

· Day three ·

L'invasion du 19

Julie Fahey

1975, en été, il fait du soleil et il fait très chaud. J'ai huit ans. Grand-père et moi sommes au jardin et prêts à choisir les légumes pour ma mère qui fait la cuisine. Elle prépare le dîner. Je touche la terre avec mes doigts et c'est froid. Je regarde l'oignon très élégant et grand. Grand-père explique le meilleur moyen de cueillir l'oignon sans l'endommager. Je dis : «Grand-père, pourquoi des pommes de terre comma ça? » Il sourit et répond : « Elles sont en terre comme ça parce que c'est mieux pour elles.»

Je me rappelle qu'on a joué à des jeux comme « cache-cache », au ballon et à « kick the can ». À six heures, nous sommes rentrés parce que c'est l'heure du dîner. Je me souviens avoir regardé ma mère qui cousait un ourlet à ma robe. C'est incroyable. Aujourd'hui, moi aussi, je sais coudre un ourlet.

Aujourd'hui, en 2020, l'invasion du 19 a juste commencé. Elle aiguise ses griffes à travers le monde entier. Il y a des millions de gens qui sont morts, elle a conquis tous les pays sous sa ceinture, comme le vent sans regret. Elle continue de faire tourner sa toile dans le monde et elle propage son virus. Y a-t-il encore de l'espoir?

Silence! Le confinement commence. Je ne peux pas travailler chez moi et je dois aller au bureau tous les jours. Le temps passe : les semaines sont devenues des mois. Notre vie est très différente et tout a changé. Il y a beaucoup de gens qui sont à la recherche de nouveaux loisirs sur internet. Ils ont appris plusieurs langues, ils font la cuisine, du jardinage, et les enfants jouent à la balle, courent dans le parc, font beaucoup d'exercice. Toutes les familles sont ensemble.

Le monde entier cherche un remède. Elle ne conquiert pas notre esprit. Elle ne bat pas notre espoir. Je suis dans mon jardin maintenant et je jardine ... Quand je touche la terre, je souris, parce que je me rappelle ce jour en 1975.

Julie's home language is English.

Memories from home

Wendy Bremang

The now-familiar skype ring tone reverberated through the living room. It was Grandad. It had just gone 16:00. That meant Grandad had finished his lunch, pottered about in the garden briefly, and had come back inside for a cup of tea and his two daily digestives, as well as a chat, of course.

Sam pressed 'accept' on the call, and there was Grandad, settled into his comfy armchair, tea in hand, digestive in his mouth. 'Good afternoon, Grandad, how are you doing?' said Sam. Grandad smiled, as he swallowed his biscuit. These daily chats between Sam and his Grandad had become a familiar and pleasant routine during Lockdown. They were now two weeks into their respective quarantines. Sam lived with his mum, who was often on shift at the local hospital, where she worked as a nurse, and Grandad lived alone.

'Afternoon Sam, me jus liming here, by meself, thinking of home,' said Grandad pensively. He had begun to talk more of Trinidad these days, often telling Sam stories of his childhood in Trinidad, where he had emigrated from as a young man almost fifty years ago. 'I miss the sea and the sun nuh Sam,' he explained. 'Now I indoors so much, me mind is far away. Yuh know today I recalled the times Tantie and me went to Maracas to sell bake. I ever tell yuh this?' Sam shook his head. 'It was a lil side hustle nah. Tantie and me, sometimes wit she children, we would jump in the van, drive to the beach and do a big cook up. We would sell coconut bake and shark at Maracas beach. There were plenty other vendors. All the women would be laughin so, tellin house business, music going. I still hear da tunes. The sound of calypso as we cooked, the sound of happiness. The sun was smiling down on us. We all be cookin, singin, eatin and enjoyin. From time to time, I would run to the sea, splash meself up and cool down, then back to cookin. Eh eh! Oh, the food so good man, me shut me eyes, I can still taste it Sam. Everythin so fresh nuh. I can even feel the soft sand and the cool waters. I miss those days Sam, tings were so simple. Nutin like all this pandemic business, Tantie would never have believe it could happen like this.'

Sam looked out of the window. It was a cloudy day. Grey. The thought of escaping this lockdown into a paradise was overwhelming. 'I hope when all of this is over, me and you can fly to Trinidad for a holiday,' said Sam. 'You have made me so hungry for some good food and some good old Trini heat.'

Grandad laughed. 'Ah fine so. That's a plan Sam. Shucks nah man, I can't wait!' Grandad smiled and full of emotion, he looked at me and said, 'Trinidad will always be special to us yuh know… it is a different world.'

Wendy's home language is English.

Andalusian dawn

Charlie Mayne

There is silence for a beat before the cicadas restart their piercing buzz. It is always the silence that throws me. Respiro profundamente, reenfocándome en el trozo de cielo nocturno andaluz que se sirve a través del tragaluz por encima de mi cabeza. Cuando agudizo los oídos, puedo distinguir fragmentos de sonido desarticulados tan débiles que casi podrían haberse imaginado. En algún lugar de la ciudad, algunos juerguistas deben haber continuado la conversación a gritos iniciada en un club nocturno.

La luz de la luna brilla con fuerza a través de la ventana. Si tuviera más energía, habría tirado la sábana y me habría vestido en esa luz como una princesa de cuento antes de arrastrarme para unirme a las personas que se divierten en la ciudad. En el fondo, sé que esta noche es para los jóvenes, y ya no soy una de ellos. Solo en la cama, el raspado de las cigarras da hachazos a los años como una navaja de barbero romano. Los recuerdos brotan con la agudeza de cincelados; su aguijón me despierta aún más. El contraste entre entonces y ahora menguando y fluyendo con el sonido de las cigarras.

El sonido de las cigarras se desvanece lentamente mientras que la luna palidece al color de una tortilla cruda frente al cielo que se ilumina a su alrededor.

'Stay in tou--', the clarion call to reach out and hit mute on whatever advert the video site's algorithm had decided fits my profile.

Out of habit, I open my email and check my other messaging apps. As expected, nothing. No point sending another message when two months' worth haven't been read by any of the recipients.

A video title catches my eye: 'Ambiance sonore - Terrasse de café à Paris: 3 HEURES'.

Quelle bonne idée ! Je mourais de soif et un café au lait, et peut-être même un croissant, me conviendraient parfaitement. Je cliquai sur le lien vidéo et, pour un instant, le silence fut flagrant. Je me mis à table et attendis un serveur.

It is always the silence that throws me.

Charlie's home language is English.

Der plätschernde Bach und el pájaro cantando

Angela McMenamin

Eines Tages ging Floss mit einer neuen Kommilitonin in dem kleinen Wald spazieren. Floss liebte es zu reden und ihre Sätze gurgelten endlos aus ihrem Mund über viele interessante Dinge. Sie sprach über Natur, Menschen, Musik, Philosophie, Essen, Reisen und alles andere, was man sich vorstellen kann. Silencia, su compañera, solo habló un poco. Principalmente solo dijo que sí o no. Floss schien es nicht zu bemerken und plapperte glücklich weiter. Der Ton ihrer Stimme klang wie der plätschernde Bach, der neben ihnen floss.

Die beiden wanderten durch die Bäume hin und her, bis sie erschöpft im Gras saßen. „Ich habe Hunger. Ich brauche dringend etwas zu essen," bemerkte Floss. „Willst du auch etwas? Ich habe Lust nach etwas wirklich Leckerem, vielleicht Sauerbraten und Knödel. Was meinst du?" Sie machte eine Pause und sah Silencia fragend an. „Na und? Was denkst du?"

Ruborizada Silencia respondió: «No lo sé.»

„Aber sicher weißt du, ob du hungrig bist und was du essen willst?"

«No lo sé.» repitió, «Lo siento.»

Floss war ratlos. Was war das denn? Diesmal schwieg sie. Silencia estaba triste y dijo: «No hablo bien como tú. Solo aprendo este idioma por poco tiempo. No sé las palabras para de los diferentes alimentos. … no entiendo nada.» y ella comenzó a llorar.

Floss sah sie erstaunt an. „Sei nicht so traurig, Silencia, ich hatte keine Ahnung, dass du mich nicht verstanden hast. Es spielt überhaupt keine Rolle, aber sag mir, warum du es mir nicht früher erzählt hast? "

Silencia respondió: «Tus palabras suenan tan bonitas y estoy avergonzada de decir mis feas palabras.»

„Deine Stimme ist wunderschön, du musst nur ein wenig üben." sagte Floss, die sich entschloss, sich jeden Tag mit Silencia zu treffen, um sich zu unterhalten.

Einige Monate später, als die Freunde wie üblich im Wald spazieren gingen, waren zwei verschiedene Stimmen zu hören. Eine klang wie der plätschernde Bach pero el otro sonaba como los pájaros en los árboles. Floss redete wieder, aber diesmal stellte sie Silencia unzählige Fragen und wartete auf die Antworten. Silencia hizo preguntas y dio opiniones con confianza. Floss war sehr stolz auf sie, aber sie erkannte auch, dass es genauso interessant war, zuzuhören wie zu sprechen. Silencia le contó historias sobre su vida y su familia y muchas otras cosas. Mit Hilfe ihrer Lehrerinnen Beatriz, Elisabeth und Silvia, lernten beide die Schönheit von Sprache und Kommunikation. Eine ganz neue Welt erschien.

Silencia dijo a Floss: «Al principio me gustaba escuchar y entendí mucho de lo que estabas diciendo, pero no podía pensar lo suficientemente rápido como para hablar, creí que pensarías que soy estúpida. Pero ahora, con práctica, tengo confianza en mí misma para hablar. Muchas gracias, Floss.»

«De nada Silencia, ahora tú puedes ayudarme. Siempre quise que mi voz sonara como un pájaro cantando.»

«Sí, por supuesto. Vamos a comer, ¿te apetece pisto con huevos o tortilla?» y el dúo wanderten weg mientras der Vogel sang con el murmullo del arroyo in perfekter armonía.

Angela's home language is English.

High hopes

Kyle Owen

I travelled home on the train that day, brimming with excitement. I'd finally landed my dream job in the city. The pay was less than I'd wanted, but it was ok, things were finally coming together. Mike waited for me at the station because the train was late getting in. I felt guilty that I hadn't told him about the interview, but I couldn't wait to see his face when I shared the great news.

I walked quickly out of the station, my heart was racing fast, there were butterflies in my belly and my palms began to sweat. This was life-changing, a new start for us after a painful year. As I closed the car door, Mike greeted me with 'Ciao Alessa'. He'd never attempted to speak my native language before; I was pleased with the effort. 'Come stai?', I replied, smiling.

'Tutto bene' he returned.

'Wow, you've been putting in some effort, where has this come from?'

'I've been learning, secretly. I wanted to surprise you,' he smiled.

'Well, surprised I am, I'll test your knowledge later. Okay, it's my turn to surprise you.'

I looked into his eyes, he was beaming, I hadn't seen him so happy in a long time. 'I have to come clean, I wasn't in work today,' I said, sheepishly.

'Oh, where were you?' He shifted forward in his seat, clamping his hands between his legs.

'At an interview, I landed a new job, my dream job. We can finally move to the city. This is a new start for us. I didn't want to tell you in case I disappointed you, but...' I was blurting it all out, he stopped me, raising his hand. He looked uncomfortable, avoiding eye contact, shifting closer and closer to the car door.

'Stop right there!' he said sharply. 'This isn't how I expected this to go, I had my own surprise. The reason I've been learning Italian is because I've got us a place out there. It's all arranged, just like we talked about. A little apartment in Florence — I've been planning it for months.' He looked at me expectantly.

We both stayed silent for what seemed like an eternity, but maybe it was only a few minutes. I felt sick, everything I'd planned was going to ruin. We both spoke at the same time, then Mike said 'Okay, you go first.'

'I can't go back to Italy, Mike. This is my home.' I fixed my gaze away from his face, I couldn't look at him.

'I have to go, it was always my dream, you knew...'

I cut him off. 'Yes, I knew, but it's too painful, I can't relive those memories, I just can't.' Tears started to stream down my face. 'We've been through too much Mike, it's either me, or Italy, you choose!' With that, he took the key out of the car, handed it to me, unbuckled his seatbelt and opened the driver's door.

'Arrivederci,' that's the last thing he said. It was over.

Kyle's home language is English.

Excentricidad

John Grierson

Debéis saber, mis nietos, que lo que es normal para una persona es excentricidad para otra.

Fue en el inverno de 1967. Volvía en autobús a la residencia universitaria después de clase en la Universidad de Edimburgo. Empezó a nevar. Vi a Adrián, un estudiante inglés, caminando por la calle sin calzado, como era su costumbre. No le importaba que nevaba. Era alto y tenía una presencia imponente, porque tenía el pelo largo y la barba larga y despeinada. Llevaba también una cruz sobre el pecho. Naturalmente, todos los estudiantes lo apodamos "Jesús".

Como sabéis, yo nací y crecí en un pueblo pequeño de las fronteras escocesas, un pueblo productor de lana. Hablamos nuestro dialecto escocés. Como en los otros pueblos fronterizos, la religión (casi) de la localidad era el rugby. Pensaba que nuestros vecinos, los Dilgers, Blythe y Dod, eran excéntricos. Había visto una vez que habían pintado el techo de su salón una mitad color magenta y la otra mitad color magnolia. No podían ponerse de acuerdo sobre el color.

—Div ee like ma ceilin? —Blythe dijo—. Aa deh like yalli, mei. Aa wantid magenta. Oo couldnae agree. Dod's a right gomerel, sometimes. The half owre Dod's heid is magenta, so aa can sei eet. Owre ma heid is magnolia so hei can sei eet.

Probablemente ellos pensaban que yo era el excéntrico. Era

estudioso, no iba a los partidos de rugby, sino a la iglesia. Sin embargo, yo no había conocido antes a una persona tan excéntrica como Adrián.

Al día siguiente, "Jesús" entró fumando un cigarrillo en la conferencia de matemáticas, aunque fumar estaba prohibido en las aulas. Se sentó en la parte delantera de la clase, frente a la profesora. Ella era joven y muy nerviosa. No podía dejar de ver la nube de humo.

—Por favor, apague el cigarrillo —pidió con timidez.

"Jesús" asintió con la cabeza, levantó el pie izquierdo y procedió a apagar el cigarrillo con la planta desnuda. Esta acción fue demasiado para la pobre profesora. Recogió sus notas y salió corriendo. La lección, claro, no se hizo ese día.

John's home languages are Greek and Scots dialect.

Les grands-parents

Aurora Ramos Varela

Cher Lecteur,

Pour vous qui lirez cette histoire, j'ai quelques questions à vous poser. Pensez-vous que toutes les personnes déjà âgées sont incapables? Qu'elles souffrent de handicap? Savent-elles gérer l'isolement et l'abandon de leur famille et de leurs amis?

Eh bien! L'histoire que je vais vous raconter est une histoire vraie qui s'est produite pendant la propagation du virus corona et la pandémie de Covid-19, qui a dévasté le monde entier d'une manière sans précédent. Et qui poursuit sans merci sa mission destructrice de démanteler impitoyablement les familles.

Au cours de cette période, il y avait deux familles qui vivaient dans un quartier près de la maison de leurs grands-parents âgés, mais à qui ils n'avaient jamais le temps de rendre visite, malgré la courte distance qui les séparait. Ils n'avaient que le temps de travailler pour la réussite de leurs entreprises. Bien que les grands-parents fussent âgés, leur vie sociale était très active, notamment parmi les jeunes, car ils aimaient partager leurs expériences de la vie et les jeunes avaient le temps de les écouter. Ils étaient très admirés et applaudis par tout le monde.

Mais soudain, quand on s'y attendait le moins, il y a eu un changement radical. Ce changement radical a affecté la vie de l'humanité, la vie de notre planète et a soulevé des questions sur notre mode de vie et nos priorités. Quand le virus corona est arrivé, les grands-parents étaient très loin de leur patrie, sur un autre continent où ils avaient de nombreux engagements et un calendrier très chargé.

En conséquence, les conférences ont été annulées, et les grands-parents n'ont pas été autorisés à retourner dans leur pays. Tout cela à cause du virus tueur. Comment combattre et affronter cet ennemi puissant et invisible? En raison de la propagation à grande échelle, faisant des milliers de victimes, tout de suite, les familles se sont souvenues de leurs grands-parents.

A cause de la dangerosité du virus mortel, le confinement à domicile a été decrété, les rassemblements publics interdits, la distanciation sociale, ainsi que le port de masque et de gants, rendus obligatoires pour arrêter la propagation de la Covid-19 et sauver des vies.

La famille d'entrepreneurs prospères, malgré la distance et la différence de fuseaux horaires, a contacté ses grands-parents sur Internet, maintenant qu'ils étaient de l'autre côté de l'océan ! Finalement, ils ont pris le temps de leur parler.

Nonobstant la situation de confinement et d'isolement social, les gens ont découvert combien il est important de réserver du temps pour la famille, car en un coup d'oeil tout peut changer de façon inattendue, sans retour. C'est peut-être trop tard. Les grands-parents étaient considérés à risque, en raison de leur âge. Malheureusement, ils ont été victimes de la Covid-19... Et le nombre de décès continue d'augmenter.

Aurora's home language is Portuguese.

The importance of being Ernesto

Liam Harrison

This has been a doozy of a day. The barney with my boss was followed by being shuffled into this dimly lit bunker, even communicating with gestures is problematic.

"¿De dónde eres tío?"

"Ma quello non parla proprio, non vale la pena dire niente."

"Il ne comprend rien."

"Δεν καταλαβαίνει σωστά."

"Das ist toll, also können wir nicht interagieren."

The interrogative voices hit me, and my grade C in GCSE French was not going to save me now.

I went for my default setting and tried to speak in English loudly, but that didn't get further than establishing my name and theirs...

Santiago Sanz Martin

Alba Errichiello

Victor Mantel

Elena Gkouzioti

Josef Hartman

And there remained the mute.

One bearded chap crouched in the corner was keeping himself to himself.

So, just to rewind…

The barney I alluded to earlier was me lambasting my bosses and, after my monologue, cataloguing their shambolic actions, warning sirens sounded all over the city and I was grabbed and put into a truck blindfolded.

After what had been maybe an hour's drive, I was pulled in the bunker.

The most multicultural bunker I had ever been in to be fair.

At least six hours passed as I observed the interactions in front of me: Santiago was able to interact a little with Victor and Alba (he was flirting particularly hard with the latter judging from the giggles) but me, Josef and Elena didn't have much conversation to warm us up.

Until finally our friend in the corner introduced himself.

"I'm Ernesto, no sé qué está pasando aquí, non ho idea di quello che sta succedendo, je suis aussi confus que vous tous quant à savoir pourquoi je suis ici, Συγγνώμη που δεν μίλησα πριν, αλλά ήμουν σε κατάσταση σοκ όπως όλοι σας, hallo an alle, ich bin nicht klüger."

After that impressive introduction, he whipped out a flask, proclaiming he had the solution to our linguistic travails.

He suggested drinking his concoction would give us the ability to all converse together.

I mean after the day I'd had, why wouldn't I just go for it?

I was the first to drink…

"Bueno, él tiene razón, funziona questa cosa, hallo… was machen wir hier? J'aimerais savoir comment nous évader. Έλενα μπορώ να πω πόσο θαυμαστής του ελληνικού πολιτισμού είμαι."

I just came out with that… it was magic.

We then proceeded to chat, albeit messily. Languages were flying about willy-nilly, but we were understanding each other, and our new best pal Ernesto had proved his word.

"Pues, eres de Córdoba, ah ok, visité una vez, es muy hermosa, cosa hai detto Alba… Venezia? No, purtroppo non l'ho visitata, ma sicuramente nel futuro lo farò." I was flying.

Interrupting our fun was a suited man who introduced himself as Aldous, he opened the bunker hatch carrying a gleeful look and ushering us to climb out.

"Welcome to a brave new world ladies and gentlemen."

Liam's home language is English.

Una pandemia pericolosa

Phelomen Mukangiliye

Tutto iniziò in Cina. Quando ne sentii parlare, nel dicembre 2019, pensai che fosse qualcosa di molto lontano e che sarebbe stato difficile che ci raggiungesse. Rimasi completamente scioccata quando, meno di tre mesi più tardi, furono dichiarati i primi casi nel Regno Unito.

All'inizio, tuttavia, rimasi abbastanza calma. Quando, però, furono attuate ulteriori misure di blocco e di distanziamento sociale, mi sentii completamente sola e la mia vita, d'un colpo, fu destabilizzata. La vita sociale, le attività collettive e gli incontri furono sospesi. Sembra siano passati decenni da quando potevo uscire senza che le mascherine mi soffocassero la faccia e senza che la paura del contatto mi affliggesse la mente. I primi due mesi si sono rivelati insopportabili. Il distacco sociale mi costringe a considerare le persone come una minaccia e gli altri vedono me allo stesso modo.

Come la maggior parte delle persone rinchiuse in casa, guardo con ammirazione i supereroi di questa guerra - i medici, gli infermieri e le infermiere nonché gli altri professionisti sanitari - munirsi dei loro dispositivi di protezione individuale (DPI) per combattere la battaglia.

Come un ladro nella notte, il Covid-19 ha portato via tutto ciò a cui più tenevamo ed ora non posso fare a meno di guardare indietro, ai giorni migliori. Sembrano un ricordo talmente lontano al punto che mi chiedo se tutto ciò sia un sogno.

Seguo costantemente gli aggiornamenti in televisione - la velocità con cui aumentano le vittime mi porta a rivivere ricordi sconvolgenti del mio passato.

Ma chi avrebbe mai pensato che questo virus avrebbe inginocchiato il mondo?!

La battaglia continua ad infuriare, ma viva è ancora in me la speranza che tutto ciò presto finisca e si torni alla normalità.

Phelomen's home language is Kinyarwanda.

Nothing is just black and now I see the golden colour on the body of a bee

Marina Traikou

These three months of home quarantine because of the pandemic outbreak have been extremely hard for Anemona. She woke up that morning and she could see the white hair on the top of her head. It seems like it appeared in one night. She made the same old movements as every day and she got dressed. Her little boy was waiting for her. However, she was not feeling the same as normal, and she looked sad, disappointed, and frightened.

Small secrets were revealed. Deep down she feels revived. She is in love. *Is not love the only thing that makes someone happy and depressed at the same time?* she thought to herself, as she was holding the bottle and gave milk to her only child.

Anemona was spending hours and hours playing and educating her little child, while working from home in the afternoons. She was a great mother, but she was also a young, beautiful, and full-of-dreams woman. *Και αν δεν πεθαίνουμε ο ένας για τον άλλον, είμαστε κιόλας νεκροί.* She keeps muttering the same phrase from her favorite Greek poet, Tasos Leivaditis: And if we don't die for each other, we are already dead. Loneliness is an extremely dangerous and addicting thing. People reveal their true selves in times of loneliness and sometimes they are pushed to live and feel hidden emotions again. Emotions that give energy and beautify someone's moments in life. This is how she wanted to feel again. Alive, wanted and in love.

While her mornings were spent at home with her son, most nights, she used to smoke some cigarettes on her balcony and have a glass of wine, while listening to her favorite music. From her balcony, Anemona could see the sea, the bay, but most importantly the colors of the sky and the games the clouds play along with the sunsets. Oh, this sunset! She has been counting the sunsets she has seen all her life. It was the calmest and most optimistic moment of the day for her.

So, that night, all her life passed before her eyes. She remembered when she was a small dark-haired girl and playing with her grandma in the backyard. The aroma of jasmine is associated with her childhood. The backyard was full of colorful flowers and the bees nestled inside them. Once, she tried to catch a bee and she looked carefully at its color. *Black and gold, like our lives* she whispered. She thought of her whole life, what she has done, the flights, the laughs, the nights out and drinks with her friends, her first love, the tears, the anxiety, everything.

I have seen so many beautiful places, I have travelled and lived across many countries, I have met all kinds of people, I have seen so many beautiful sunsets and I am extremely blessed and thankful for each and every moment in my life. I am not weak, I am not empty, I shouldn't be scared! she said loudly, as if she was talking to someone. *Love is hard and painful. How I miss a walk on the beach and a movie in a summer open air cinema with a beer in hand, like when we were teenagers*, she continued.

Things will find a way to return to normality and people will get used to the new reality, but some things will never change and will always be the same, only to remind us that we are still humans and that we need to feel. To feel the love and the pain and rise again each day like the sun does before the sunset.

Marina's home language is Greek.

Santo Cebo

Al Wood

Todos estaban activos esa noche: las aves, los cuerpos, los cadáveres desmembrados. Algunos cantaban, regocijándose en la sangre manchada en sus manos; otros se peleaban. Algunos flexionaban sus caras y mandíbulas delante de los demás, mientras brujas murmuraban palabras satánicas. Unos pocos rezagados se arrastraban como entrañas hacia los oscuros alrededores que envuelven la ciudad. Sí, fue una noche perfectamente macabra en Santo Cebo.

Él llevaba todo un año esperando ese día para la misión que se avecinaba. Pero en medio del caos, había perdido a su camarada. Sólo tenía que mantener la calma. Tenía que llegar al punto de seguridad. Estaba inquieto, pero no nervioso; conocía el procedimiento.

Pero ¿en quién se podía confiar por aquí? Nadie, no hables con nadie, eso es lo que le habían instruido desde hacía tiempo. Bueno, eso no era cierto. A veces se paraban a charlar con otros desconocidos vestidos con ropas sencillas y eran momentos alegres. «Pero no se podía confiar en él para distinguir lo confiable de lo sospechoso», decían, «al menos no todavía. Así que no confíes en nadie».

Aunque él mismo tenía dudas sobre sus instrucciones, la lógica o la falta de ella, vivía de su mando. Mas ahora, se encontró entendiendo su orden mientras intentaba navegar por el mar de animales esa noche.

Los cuerpos alargados deambulaban ante él. Uno de ellos se topó con él; él se estremeció. «Esto está bien», piensa, «no mencionaron nada sobre chocar con otros».

Mirando de reojo había uno merodeando, acechándolo. Lo sintió acercarse a él primero antes de verlo echarse hacia adelante, deslizándose hacia él. Las palmas de sus manos se humedecieron y los latidos de su corazón se elevaron cuando el pánico se apoderó de él. Se puso a caminar más rápido. Pero la muchedumbre se lo tragó y mientras empujaba y luchaba para escapar de el agobio, la figura se abalanzó hacia adelante, hasta que sintió una mano fría y húmeda en su cuello.

—¿Adónde vas? —dijo la figura.

Se dio la vuelta. Vislumbró brevemente el cuerpo asqueroso antes de soltar un chillido que lo sorprendió. Los demonios cercanos se giraron hacia él. Le entró el pánico. Corrió. Algunos trataron de bloquearlo gritando «¿Con quién estás?», pero siguió corriendo.

Vio el punto de encuentro. ¡Por fin! Se sintió aliviado mientras se abrazaban, una sonrisa de exuberancia se le escapó en el momento de bajar la guardia mientras su compañera lo saludaba abiertamente y lloraba de alegría. Ella era demasiado emocional, pero a veces era entrañable.

Por suerte, habían perdido los fantasmas. Unos fantasmas los habían alcanzado, pero tan pronto como los ojos de ellos se encontraron con los de su compañera, se fueron. Como dice el dicho, «Hay seguridad en el grupo».

Ahora podía seguir adelante con la misión. Se sintió más fuerte al avanzar con su aliada, saber que ella estaba allí le dio una sensación de seguridad. Juntos se acercaron a una casa antigua.

—¡Truco o trato! —él gritó.

Su madre se avergonzaba mientras una multitud de dulces se vertían en su bolsa de calabaza.

Al's home language is English.

· Day four ·

Achos fy nhad: por Franco

Peter Bradley

Gyrrodd y pâr ifanc heibio i Toulouse gan anelu tuag at y de. Y dyn oedd yn sedd y gyrrwr: ifanc, cyhyrog a golygus. Wrth ei ochr eisteddai merch ifanc, pryd tywyll. Gwenon nhw'n gariadus ar ei gilydd bob hyn a hyn.

'Roedd hi'n ddwy awr yn ddiweddarach, wedi dwys holi'r hwn a holi'r llall mewn pentrefi uniaith – ble mai'r unig Saesneg ar wefusau'r trigolion oedd enwau pel-droedwyr Lloegr: Bobby Moore, Jackie Charlton, Nobby Stiles – sut i gael hyd i'r tŷ, o'r diwedd llusgon nhw eu bagiau trwy'r drws.

'Doedd yna ddim rhyw lawer o chwant bwyd arnyn nhw a hithau mor boeth, felly cymeron nhw botelaid o gwrw'r un – rhy gynnes ar ôl oriau yng nghist y car – i'w yfed ar y patio. Roedd haul Mehefin ar fachlud ac yn dangos eira copaon y mynyddoedd yn goch.

"Mae'r mynyddoed bach yn fwy nag s'gynnon ni adra'" meddai'r ferch.

"Be'? Y Pyrenees? Ydyn".

"Pam na chroeswn ni'm i mewn i Sbaen? Maen nhw'n deud ei bod hi'n braf yna".

"Na, byth".

"Pam lai?"

"Achos fy nhad ac achos Franco".

"Sut?"

"Tra bo Franco yna, a thra bo 'nhad, 'd a' i byth i Sbaen".

Wythnos yn ddiweddarach, troeson nhw tua'r dwyrain: am yr Eidal. Yr oedd Mussolini wedi marw, wedi'r cwbl.

El equipo de voluntarios se sentó a la mesa para la cena, frente a las montañas que formaban una cortina negra, ocultando el horror de la fosa de los ojos de los franceses. El sol se ponía lentamente y, por solo un instante, las cumbres pirenaicas se tintaron de rojo.

Entre los comensales, se sentaba un hombre que tenía pinta de ser mucho más viejo que los otros. Era un hombre fuerte y estaba claro que se había cuidado: guapo, quizás, en su día. El viejo dirigió sus ojos hacia la jefa de los arqueólogos – una joven catalana con pelo largo y tez oscura, misteriosa – protegiéndose los ojos del sol con la mano. Le recordaba a otra joven de hacía muchos años.

—¿Tú, Geraint, por qué decidiste cavar aquí? —le preguntó la chica dirigente.

—Por mi padre y por Franco.

—¿Cómo?

Le pareció muy raro relatar esta vieja historia a una chica tan recién llegada al mundo. ¿Cómo podía explicarle a ella la decepción en la cara paterna, mientras moría de cáncer en la cama hospitalaria? Perdiendo poco a poco la vida. Una vida luchada y una vida derrotada, a cada paso. Tomó un profundo respiro antes de continuar:

—Mi padre luchó no muy lejos de aquí. Me hizo jurar que nunca visitaría España mientras Franco siguiera vivo.

—¿Y ahora qué?

—El viejo ya está bajo tierra. Franco también.

—¿Y la lucha se ha acabado?

—La lucha, no. Eso, no.

Peter's home languages are Welsh and English.

Fireflies

Alyona Campbell

'Bioluminescence occurs in all sorts of creatures but also in terrestrial arthropods such as fireflies. Bioluminescence is generated by luciferin, a light-emitting compound found in such organisms' – Krishna's susurrant voice rattled to Jennie and Alyona who were melting under the spell of the 'flying fairies' as they called the fireflies. It was late evening and the trio sat under canopy of a mature mango tree in the foothills of Himalayas. They sat there till the light began to fail, observing rose-ringed parakeets with their distinct green colour, chanting, subvocalizing tacit prayers each in their own way, sharing life stories in all honesty. They felt they were gaining proficiency in eye and ear worshipping. All they had to do is simply to be there, to be present, and the magic was not late in coming...

'These different species use their own code of flashes to communicate in search of their perfect half during the breeding season. Imagine, the female mimics the flashes of another species in order to attract a male...and eats him up!' - continued Krishna with a laugh. Jennie laughed heartily at Krishna's idiosyncratic character. Something in his words made Alyona's spine crawl. Just then the music began to play, the nocturnal drum ritual. At that moment Jagmohan, the owner of the farm, came and sat next to her with his gaze piercing even under the moonlight. She breathlessly cupped her hands at his request and he placed a firefly on her palms, silently letting his eyes focus on her. Alyona's inner tempest and need of grounding evoked memories of the wonderful smell one enjoys with the rain after a period of dry weather. *'Petrichor, petrichor, petrichor...'* – the thought played voicelessly the word over and over in her mind in order to catch her breath. She was grateful when Krishna's voice interrupted her impromptu mantra.

'Mangifera Indica, or otherwise a flowering tree mango. According to Vedic myth, the daughter of the Sun god, Surya, was reborn as a mango and the King of the land had fallen in love and united with her...Buddha always rested under a mango tree and since his time the mango tree was considered as a wish-fulfilling tree...' They closed their eyes and took deep breaths. Drums continued in the background; fireflies continued their mesmerising enchantment.

Jennie and Krishna bid their goodnights and took their leave. Jagmohan stood up, said good night but has not moved a foot observing Alyona's inability to conceal sadness and internal struggle of moral dilemma. She knew he knew. She looked at the fireflies in the distance and raised her eyes to look at him. The drums stopped short. *Silence can be so tangible,* she thought. 'Do you want a hug?' – he asked. They stared at each other without moving for a while. She said 'yes'.

Alyona's home language is Russian.

Un autre monde

Janet Holt

Ann, Guenièvre and Letitia

Ann walked across the field, trepidation building as she approached the horses. A retired farmer, she still had two broodmares: Guenièvre, an elegant Selle Français whose size belied her gentleness, and Letitia, an excitable Spanish Lipizzaner who disliked humans and who was always ready to bite or kick. They were preparing to foal, but everyone was in lockdown because of the virus and Ann was on her own. Thunder rolled around the sky prophesying catastrophe.

Un débat multiculturel

—¡Está aquí de nuevo! Letitia regarda avec dédain la femme qui approchait.

Guenièvre rit en se rappelant hier soir quand elles avaient fait une blague à Ann, faisant semblant d'être en travail. Elles avaient gémi et avaient maugré chaque fois qu'Ann apparaissait, imitant les sons de deux naissances imminentes. Ann s'était gratté la tête, revenant chaque heure pendant que les juments se payaient sa tête.

— Elle ne te veut pas de mal, Letitia. Écoute-la parler !

—¡Escucharla! ¡Escucharla! ¡No quiero! Ella habla inglés y me ofende los oídos. Es peor que escucharte hablar francés todo el día. ¿Por qué no hablan español? Es el idioma más hermoso del mundo.

— Non ! Non ! Non ! Le français est meilleur, il est précis et sans ambiguïté.

—¡Es ininteligible! El español es ardiente e intenso.

— Mais le français est poétique et romantique. C'est le langage de l'amour !

—Creo que eso es italiano. ¡Justo lo que necesitamos – una cuarta lengua!

Tandis que les juments riaient, Guenièvre ressentit les premières contractions.

P-day : les poulinières poulinent

Guenièvre laissa Ann inspecter son poulain, né sans problème une heure avant. Guenièvre tressaillit soudainement de peur. À quelques mètres d'elle, Letitia était couchée sur le sol et gémissait. La jambe droite de son poulain était pliée vers l'arrière, empêchant la mise-bas. Elle vit Ann s'agenouiller pour essayer de redresser la patte du poulain, mais Letitia se tendit et empêcha la manœuvre.

Ann tried desperately to remember a few Spanish words:

—Por favor Letitia, deje de empujar.

Guenièvre retint son souffle. Letitia était tellement surprise d'entendre des mots espagnols qu'elle se détendit et Ann redressa rapidement la jambe du poulain. Détectant l'amélioration, Letitia donna une ultime poussée énorme et son poulain naquit. Guenièvre fut soulagée. Letitia se leva et examina son nouveau-né. Ann s'éloigna d'elle de quelques mètres très rapidement, mais elle n'avait rien à craindre. Letitia la regardait avec reconnaissance et, pour la première fois, ses oreilles étaient en avant dans un geste d'amitié. Leurs regards se croisèrent. Ann sourit et partit. Guenièvre n'en croyait pas ses yeux !

Only Fools and Horses

The storm passed and the morning sun peeped out from behind a cloud with the promise of a fine day. Ann stood at the gate, exhausted but happy. She looked across the field at a scene from a Stubbs painting: the two mares standing, utterly content, as their new foals played together. Yes, she thought, this was 2020 and, since the arrival of Covid19, it was a different world. Fortunately, one thing was the same – the everlasting miracle of new life.

Janet's home language is English.

Under the rainbow - 在彩虹下

Steven Whall

在2020年，世界将永远改变。不是因为战争或饥荒，而是因为据认为是起源于中国武汉的病毒。它迅速传播到世界各地，极易传染，使最脆弱的人群处于危险之中。

全球人们被迫留在家中，以防止疾病传播和挽救生命。世界各国不确定如何应对这一瘟疫的爆发。

尽管有死亡和经济衰退的景象，以前从未经历过瘟疫的国家之间已经形成一种社区意识。

这种被称为"冠状病毒"的疾病可以感染所有人，目前，科学家正在研发和测试疫苗，以消除这种未知的感染，据信这种感染是从动物身上转移过来的。

这种悲惨的局势产生了意想不到的结果。公众感谢那些低薪的社工，他们冒着生命危险为社区服务，以便继续提供治疗。

自从隔离以来，人们需要努力互相支持，并理解和欣赏彼此的差异，所以就产生了社区和同情心。

彩虹象征着世界范围的重大变化，被描绘成希望的象征, 雨的尽头和阳光的开始。各大洲第一次相互关注并相互支持，因为每个国家处于这一大流行的不同阶段，国际间的团结正在建立。

此外，我们注意到了一些不公正现象，并正在逐步走向平等。在美国发生的事件凸显了种族群体之间仍然存在的歧视和偏见。

社会正在发展成为一个统一的族群，即人类。在彩虹下和谐共处，互相庆祝。

Steven's home language is English.

L'Amour au temps du coronavirus

Irena Peczak

Sally est assise dans sa voiture. Ses papiers de travail sont éparpillés partout dans sa voiture. Elle s'en fiche. Elle sent le sang battre dans ses veines. Il ne lui reste que quelques heures. Aujourd'hui, David sort de l'hôpital. Il y a deux mois, il a été hospitalisé pour le Covid 19. Elle se rappelle leur dernière querelle. Ils ne se sont jamais insultés aussi grossièrement : « *you fat cow* » ; « *you callous bastard* ». Maintenant ces mots sont dénués de sens. Un souvenir lui a traversé l'esprit – David dans son pyjama préféré : « *I solemnly swear that I am up to no good* ». Elle a souri mais c'était un sourire plutôt amer et douloureux.

Sally est consciente qu'elle a l'air fatigué et désordonné. Elle admet qu'elle ne peut pas rivaliser avec cette autre femme. Toutefois, la seule chose dont elle se soucie en ce moment est comment expliquer aux enfants qu'elle revient de l'hôpital sans leur père.

C'est l'automne dernier que Sally a trouvé la photo de l'autre femme. Sur la photo, David tenait une femme élégante et mince par la taille ; derrière eux de grands mots : Cambridge Shakespeare Festival. On pouvait lire au dos de la photo : « *Love comforteth like sunshine after rain. Sophie xx* ». Sally est prête à la rencontrer ; la haine a disparu au moment où David a été diagnostiqué avec le coronavirus. Depuis, elle ne pense qu'à lui et à leurs enfants.

Sophie est assise dans un avion et tortille un morceau de papier dans sa paume. Elle n'a pas besoin de le lire, elle connaît les mots par cœur. On dirait qu'il y a mille ans qui ont passé, depuis qu'elle a vu pour la dernière fois cette étrange langue écrite de la même écriture griffonnée... Ses pensées sont interrompues par une annonce d'atterrissage. Sophie a pris une profonde inspiration sous son masque en pensant qu'avec les masques, ce serait la façon la plus bizarre de rencontrer David et sa femme. Elle n'a pas hâte de faire cette rencontre, mais elle le lui a promis.

Elle est arrivée devant l'hôpital, mais de plus en plus Sophie se rend de compte que c'est une erreur, elle n'aurait pas dû venir ici. Elle cherchait l'entrée quand elle a vu un étrange couple d'âge moyen, leurs corps entrelacés, ils avaient tous les deux l'air épuisé, ils pleuraient... Sophie les regarde et elle reconnaît soudain David. Des larmes coulaient de ses yeux mais étrangement elle se sentait heureuse. Elle a sorti le morceau de papier et a relu : « *Schatzi, kannst du mir jemals vergeben ?* ».

Sophie pouvait entendre son cœur battre fort, elle regarde de nouveau David et pour la dernière fois elle se souvient d'avoir frappé avec impatience à sa porte tout en citant fièrement Alfred de Musset dans un français parfait : « *Il faut qu'une porte soit ouverte ou fermée.* » Elle ouvre son portable et tape très lentement quatre lettres : NEIN.

Irena's home language is Czech.

El anciano y el libro sagrado

Nawell Nother

Un día de verano, un anciano estaba sentado al lado de un arroyo que atravesaba su jardín. Casi siempre, pasaba un buen momento del día contemplando la naturaleza y leyendo su libro. Un libro que conservaba con mucho amor. Según él, el único recuerdo que guarda de sus abuelos españoles que llegaron a la isla hace muchos años. En la mañana, llega su nieto, intrigado porque su abuelo leía el mismo libro día tras día y le pregunta:

—Abuelo, ¿por qué lees tu libro sagrado todos los días? ¡Intenté leerlo varias veces, pero nunca entiendo lo que está escrito en este libro!

El abuelo se toma su tiempo antes de contestar al pequeño:

—Me traes la cesta vacía que está encima del montón de carbón y te explicaré mi respuesta.

El nieto obedece y trae la canasta al abuelo.

El niño pregunta:

—¿Qué quieres hacer? la cesta está sucia con polvo de carbón.

El abuelo contesta:

—Lo sé mi niño, ahora vas a ir al arroyo y la llenas de agua, después me la traes.

El niño desahuciado obedece al abuelo. Diez minutos después, el nieto regresa con la cesta vacía y dice:

—¡Esto no tiene ningún sentido, es imposible!

El abuelo contesta:

—Lo sé hijo mío, hazlo otra vez y ¡lo entenderás más tarde!

Otra vez el niño, contrariado, vuelve al arroyo para traer el agua. Esta vez vuelve enojado y se sienta al lado de su abuelo sin decir una palabra. El abuelo empieza a hablarle:

—Mira hijo mío, sé que no ves el sentido de esta prueba. Lo que quería enseñarte era al mismo tiempo mi respuesta a tu pregunta.

El niño sigue escuchando al abuelo con curiosidad. El abuelo continúa:

—Cuando leo mi libro aún no lo entiendo a veces, pero me purifica por dentro cada día y me calma el alma.

El niño le pregunta:

—Pero ¿cómo abuelo?

El abuelo le contesta:

—Yo soy igual que la cesta que no puede contener el agua, el hecho de leer mi libro sagrado sin entender el sentido profundo de algunas palabras tiene un efecto interior divino. Ahora mira la cesta, ¿cómo la ves?

El niño contesta:

—Está más limpia.

El abuelo le dice:

—¿Te das cuenta ahora que cuando leo mi libro sagrado es más para purificarme que para entenderlo?

Nawell's home language is French.

Aufgewacht

Lindsey Budge

4. Dezember 2020

Beep... Beep... Beep...

Ich öffne die Augen.

„Hallo!? Können Sie mich hören? Wie heißen Sie? Können Sie mir Ihren Namen sagen? Wissen Sie, wo Sie sind?"

Alles ist zu laut, zu leuchtend, zu viel...

... ich schließe wieder die Augen.

8. März 2021

Also, anscheinend bin ich in den letzten 14 Monaten in einem tiefen Koma gewesen. Es gab einen Unfall, als ich nach der Arbeit nach Hause zurückfuhr. Ich weiß nicht was passiert ist, aber anscheinend habe ich viel Glück, dass ich noch lebe.

Ich fühle mich jetzt viel besser, aber ich habe noch viel zu tun. Ich muß wieder laufen lernen, aber ich habe keine Sorgen darüber; ich werde wieder ein normales Leben führen.

Das Leben allgemein ist jedoch anders. Die Welt heutzutage ist ungleich der Welt, an die ich mich vor dem Koma erinnere. Die fühlt sich beinahe fremd an.

Ich verstehe, dass viel passiert ist, seit ich schlief. Es gab die Pandemie – Covid-19. Viele waren infiziert, viele sind gestorben. Fast die ganze Welt war geschlossen. Es gab Sperren überall, die

Leute mussten zu Hause bleiben. Ich könnte es mir nicht vorstellen. Jetzt ist es meistens vorbei, es gibt noch ein paar Ausbrüche ab und zu, aber sie sind schnell aufgehoben.

Es gibt aber Unterschiede überall. Feine Unterschiede, die ich überall sehe. Manchmal wundere ich mich, ob ich die einzige bin, die diese Unterschiede merkt.

Am auffälligsten sind die Vögel, es gibt viel mehr als vorher und sie sind so laut, so gesprächig, so fröhlich. Dieser Virus hat ihr Leben zum Guten verändert. Ich habe keine Ahnung wieso, aber es ist unmissverständlich. Es freut mich so.

Ich sehe auch einen Unterschied zwischen den Menschen. Sie unterhalten sich miteinander anders. Die Beziehungen haben sich geändert. Es ist schwer zu beschreiben, aber es ist als ob sie einen neuen Respekt für einander haben. Ich sehe es besonders mit Familien. Es gibt mehr Geduld, mehr Akzeptanz, mehr Verständnis, mehr Fröhlichkeit. Sie scheinen engere Beziehungen miteinander zu haben.

Für 12 Wochen mussten alle zu Hause bleiben. Sie konnten einmal pro Tag nach draußen gehen um frische Luft zu bekommen. Einige Leute mussten noch arbeiten, aber viele waren von der Arbeit beurlaubt. Sie mussten mit den Kindern Heimunterricht machen. Sie haben zusammen gebacken, Brettspiele gespielt, viel zusammen gelesen. Für viele war es wie zwölf Wochen voller Sonntage. Sie hatten eine große Pause erfahren.

Es gefällt mir, diese Umwandlung. Früher waren die Leute zu beschäftigt und viel zu gestresst. Die Leute lebten nicht im Moment. Ich glaube, die Menschen haben jetzt die Hauptprioritäten des Lebens erkannt. Was das Wichtigste ist? Nicht Geld oder die Arbeit, sondern die Gesundheit, die Familie, die Freunde, zusammen miteinander Zeit zu verbringen. Zeit in der Natur zu verbringen. Mit den Kindern zu spielen. Präsent in ihrem Leben zu sein.

Ich glaube die Menschheit brauchte diese Pause. Wahr ist es, dass viele gestorben sind und dass das schrecklich ist. Aber was ist der Sinn des Lebens, wenn man es nicht genießen kann? Jetzt ist die Menschheit aufgewacht.

Ich freue mich, dass ich in dieser Welt auch aufgewacht bin.

Lindsey's home language is English.

El verdadero viaje

Maike Albus

Desde niña había viajado por todo el mundo, pero esta vez, su viaje sería diferente.

Tomó el tren desde París hasta Le Puy. Visitó a su amigo, quien le sugirió empezar el Camino de Santiago por la "via Podiensis". Su amigo le dijo:

« Mais bien sûr, tu dois commencer au Puy-en-Velay où je suis né et où je vis encore maintenant ! »

Alors, allí estaba y había llegado el día de la partida.

Se encontraba tranquila consigo misma y con su entorno. Naturalmente, meditaba diariamente y era la meditación lo que le daba el equilibrio completo, el amor y la paz interior.

Andando, no se daba cuenta de que le dolían los pies. Estaba alegre de estar viva. Era fácil vivir en el presente, sin la perturbación de los pensamientos que vienen del pasado o del futuro. Ella vivía simplemente, en la realidad, veía las cosas como eran, no quería analizar nada ni a nadie.

Pasó por varios maravillosos paisajes y aldeas. Un día hacía sol, otro día llovía y otros días hacía un viento terrible y casi dejó de caminar porque era un esfuerzo enorme continuar. Sin embargo, siempre estaba gozosa. Se había dado cuenta de que este camino representa una experiencia espiritual para muchos peregrinos. Encontraba a personas de todas las edades y culturas; todas esperaban que algo especial sucediera durante su camino. Como un gran logro, un estallido o una luz interior que se enciende de pronto…, cuando se acerca el final del camino.

Había conocido a muchos buscadores de la verdad. Tenían interés por saber más.

Mirando la ribera, el bosque, las colinas o sentados en el albergue, les daba su realización del ser así:

The pilgrims sit quietly with their hands on Mother Earth, eyes closed, attention inside. She asks them to

place their right hand on the heart and the left on their knee. With full concentration on the heart, they affirm:

'Mother, I am the spirit!'

« Mère, je suis l´esprit ! »

Next, they put their right hand on the top of their head. They press down their hand and rotate the scalp seven times clockwise. With attention here, they humbly ask:

'Mother, please may I have my self-realization?'

« Mère, s´il Vous plaît, donne moi la réalisation du soi ! »

Finally, they lift their hand up, above their head. There, they feel for something; a cool or a warm breeze perhaps. They take their hand down and place it on the right leg.

—Mantén la atención encima de la cabeza sin pensar en nada. Cuando lleguen pensamientos, solo obsérvalos y déjalos pasar.

Their focus remains on top of their heads for a few minutes more. There is absolute silence, awareness and bliss within.

Con amor en el corazón expresaron su gratitud:

—Que sigas muy bien y God bless!

Finalmente, llegó a Santiago y luego al fin de la tierra, a Finisterre. Pero todavía faltaba mucho para llegar al fin de su evolución, al fin del verdadero camino interior.

Maike's home language is German.

Un monde différent

Catriona Reoch

Il fait si froid. Au coeur des montagnes, le vent hurle comme un loup dans la nuit et le vieil homme frissonne dans sa houppelande légère. Il a peur de ne pas achever sa tâche. Il ferme les yeux et essaie de dormir. Les grandes roches sont son lit et le ciel glacial est sa couverture.

Le matin arrive et il recommence son voyage lentement, lentement vers sa destination. Il marche tout le jour. Les montagnes dominent de très haut le petit homme, et elles portent les premières neiges de l'hiver. Le soir, il trouve un lieu abrité où il fait du feu et il regarde profondément les flammes. Il se souvient des mots de son maître. « Trouve le beau lieu et cache le trésor. Si les ombres sont sombres et les roches sont pâles, le lieu est bon. Ne me déçois pas, mon vieil ami. » Mais maintenant son maître est mort. Il sait qu'il porte un petit objet doré et caché mais il ne sait pas ce que c'est. Son maître a lui dit que l'objet contenait les espoirs et les rêves de l'avenir mais il ne le comprend pas.

Le jour d'après, le vieux descend dans une vallée verte. Le bon lieu. Dans un petit bois, il trouve des roches plates avec des raies de quartz blanc entre le granit noir. Il s'arrête et il écoute pendant un moment. C'est le silence à part les oiseaux dans les arbres. Une brindille casse net soudain et il commence à se dépêcher. En creusant dans la terre il enfouit le colis sous les roches anciennes. Sa peau picote et il se tourne rapidement, mais il est trop tard. Le coup est dur et rapide et il tombe lourdement. Le sang coule de son oreille et l'agresseur se retire, contrarié, parce que pour une raison ou pour une autre le grand homme ne peut pas trouver le paquet caché. Le trésor est en sûreté dans sa tombe terreuse.

500 ans plus tard

La silence de la vallée verte est détruit par les hurlements des hommes. Le soleil brille et les oiseaux chantent et tout est très bucolique jusqu'à ce qu'ils trouvent quelque chose de sinistre. Un crâne humain. C'est vieux, vraiment, mais c'est inquiétant tout le même. Les autorités sont alertées et la gendarmerie, les scientifiques de médecine légale et les archéologues arrivent.

Ils enquêtent sur le site et ce n'est pas qu'un crâne. C'est un squelette complet, et oui, c'est très vieux. Il y repose depuis 500 ans et la fêlure dans le crâne montre qu'il a été tué par quelqu'un de fort et de grande taille. Très mystérieux.

Les hommes quittent la vallée verte et quand ils disparaissent, le silence retourne au petit bois au coeur des montagnes. Le soleil se couche et dans les derniers rayons de la lumière étincelante, quelque chose luit entre les roches noires et blanches.

C'est un monde différent, mais le trésor reste à l'abri des mains méchantes des hommes ignorants. Prions pour qu'il reste comme ça, enterré dans sa tombe terreuse.

Catriona's home language is English.

Prima della fine del Carnevale

C. Emmett

Se viaggi a Venezia e non sei gravato dal denaro superfluo, starai a Mestre. Questo è un quartiere a nord della città, dove si trovano i dormitori economici. È sulla terraferma e inizialmente rimarrai delusa, ma solo per poco tempo. Per puro caso, sei arrivata non molto tempo prima del Carnevale. Sarà il caos, te lo dicono tutti. Bedlam! Ma devi vedere tu stessa, decidi.

E così, in una mattina di febbraio, uscirai dalla tua accogliente cuccetta. Troverai nell'assoluto silenzio della camerata dei vestiti puliti nel tuo zaino e passerai di soppiatto davanti ai tuoi compagni di dormitorio russanti. Oggi sorseggi il tuo caffè e aggrotti le sopracciglia alla notizia. Questa nuova malattia; how awful. Ti chiedi se sarà contenuta, come la SARS, o se potrebbe diffondersi. Speri di no.

Sei vicino alla stazione: flotte di barche e tram, treni e autobus ti aspettano per portarti a Venezia. Scegli il treno perché è il meno sconcertante. Il treno ti trasporta, ti allontana dal cemento grigio, lontano dagli hotel della catena e dai parcheggi; ti porta lungo il Ponte della Libertà e sopra le acque della Laguna Veneta. Esci dalla stazione, sbattendo le palpebre alla luce del sole.

Sei vicina alle lacrime, all'improvviso. Questo è un tuo sogno sin da quando eri bambina: una città costruita su una laguna, canali per le strade. Una città che ha visto guerre, intrighi, pestilenze e ogni sorta di distruttore, eppure è sopravvissuta. Le persone a cui hai parlato del tuo sogno sogghignano; un posto così piccolo, dicono. Lì tutto sarebbe stato umido e i canali sporchi avrebbero puzzato. Sei venuta a diffidare della tua fantasia.

Ma ora sei qui, e i canali odorano solo di acqua di fiume: sono i turchesi più incantevoli. Gli edifici sono aggraziati come li immaginavi. Riconosci la cupola verde della Chiesa San Simeon Piccolo sull'altro lato del Canal Grande, il Ponte degli Scalzi a sinistra.

Trascorri quasi tutti i giorni semplicemente inciampando per la città. Ti arrampichi su e giù per i ponti e serpeggi per le strade strette, sbirciando fra le finestre chiuse e fermandoti a raccogliere inezie per la gente a casa. Sei spinta dalla folla ma ci pensi poco. L'artrite ti tiene lontana da molte delle principali attrazioni, così ti accontenti di piccoli musei e gallerie nascosti nelle stradine secondarie. Quando sei stanca, ti fermi in un bar per un caffè o uno spritz, o ti siedi in una delle piazzette sorseggiando una San Pellegrino.

Dopo il tramonto, ti trovi sul Ponte degli Scalzi, meravigliandoti dei festaioli mascherati e in costume sotto un'enorme luna piena, il colore del rame. Sì, è il caos - ma il caos è bellissimo.

Alla fine, devi partire prima che finisca il Carnevale; i tuoi fondi non dureranno molto. Ti incammini verso la stazione per l'ultima volta, con immensa tristezza.

Giorni dopo, di nuovo in Inghilterra, apprendi che il Carnevale è finito presto comunque. Una nuova peste è arrivata a La Serenissima. Ancora una volta, sei vicina alle lacrime.

C. Emmett's home language is English.

Love in Der Schweiz

Rachael Garston

I was in my thirteenth year as an expat in Asia when I was reassigned to Switzerland.

My time in Asia was the best. Full of vibrancy and colour. Fragrance and flavour. The weekends always began with local Hawker food and live music on Fridays, designer shopping on Saturdays, and ended with five-star Sunday champagne brunches. Then to re-enter the brutally competitive workforce again Monday. I LOVED it.

As I took the taxi ride to the small town I was to call home I quickly realised this was not going to be the same five-star life I had left behind.

The following months went from bad to worse, as did the weather. By February people were adamant I should take up skiing. 'Try it' they said, 'you will love it' they said. So, in a vain attempt to find enjoyment in the season I hit the slopes. It was just not meant to be! As soon as I started to move I realised to my terror that I couldn't stop. Ending up in a heap at the bottom I decided very quickly it wasn't for me!

Halfway through my second year things hadn't improved. My neighbours despised me for many reasons, the worst being that I didn't speak enough 'Schweizer Deutsch' for their liking. Then I met Lee. Now Lee was my type of gal. We enjoyed the same food, shared the same philosophies, and above all, she understood my pain!

One evening over dinner I asked her 'So how did you grow to like Switzerland so much?'

'That's easy. You need to go to the mountains.' She replied simply. I shared the story of my disastrous skiing event, and she laughed. 'Not skiing' she replied. 'That's not enjoying the mountains... Hiking!'.

'Lee, it's really not my thing.' I replied.

'Just come with me and once you play in the mountains, I promise you will love it here forever. Just like Heidi.' She laughed.

A month later I found myself dutifully following Lee up the WanderWeg trail towards the summit of one of the many mountains in Kanton Schwyz.

After the hardest four hours of my life, we finally reached the peak! There I found myself surrounded by fluffy white clouds. Reaching up, I felt I could almost touch the bright yellow sun which was set against the clearest blue sky. Forests of the white peaks lay all around us as far as the eye could see.

While descending my mind was completely quiet and perfectly still. Every burden, every grievance which I had carried up the mountain with me, and God knows I was heavy, had dissolved.

'Shall we go somewhere else next weekend?' Lee asked once we had reached the base.

'Would love to' I replied. Her mission accomplished.

And she was right! Once I had discovered the Swiss mountains I have never wanted to leave!

Rachael's home language is English.

L'escalier

Angela Gibson

J'avais aperçu la vieille dame plusieurs fois depuis mon emménagement dans la maison Belle Epoque un peu délabrée. C'était une femme maigre habillée en noir, au visage pâle et aux cheveux longs et gris. Chaque fois qu'elle me voyait, elle rentrait dans son appartement en vitesse.

Le soir, je pensais entendre quelqu'un jouer du piano – les *Préludes* de Debussy peut-être - mais la musique me semblait très lointaine.

Puis, un jour elle m'a arrêtée et m'a dit ce récit d'une voix claire et haute :

« C'est mon anniversaire. J'ai quatre-vingt-dix ans. C'est *incroyable*, n'est-ce pas ? Il y a soixante-seize ans que j'habite cet appartement.

Auguste, mon mari, et moi, nous sommes tous les deux, tombés amoureux de l'escalier. Regardez, c'est comme la spire d'un coquillage parfait ! En le montant pour la première fois jusqu'au quatrième étage, nous nous sommes sentis comme des âmes célestes sur le point de rencontrer une divinité très élégante, et certainement pas un agent immobilier un peu débraillé. Auguste a signé le contrat sans la moindre hésitation, en oubliant sur le moment l'existence de mon piano demi-queue.

Chaque fois que je descendais l'escalier, les notes fines et ondulantes des *Gymnopédies* de Satie jouaient dans mon esprit et même quand je portais un vieil imperméable pour aller au marché, c'était comme si je portais un manteau du soir, signé Paul Poiret.

Mais il est devenu beaucoup plus difficile de monter les quatre étages avec deux enfants, les courses et un landau…

Un soir, après qu'Auguste m'a dit des mots particulièrement cruels, de désespoir, j'ai regardé la cage de l'escalier d'en haut, mais en voyant sa beauté vertigineuse, j'ai pensé à Maria Callas, sublime dans le rôle de Tosca quand elle chante 'Vissi d'Arte', et toute ma douleur s'en est trouvé transformée en art !

Quand Auguste est mort, cette tragédie est devenue une farce, quand quatre hommes ont essayé de descendre son cercueil. Cette manœuvre a été presque plus difficile que quand on a déménagé mon piano !

Sans doute, les cent marches me donnaient de l'exercice – quand j'étais jeune. Mais actuellement, il ne me reste aucun cartilage dans les genoux. Tout ce que je désire maintenant, c'est un *ascenseur* ! »

J'ai répondu qu'il fallait célébrer cet anniversaire merveilleux ! De plus, j'ai dit que je l'aiderais à demander l'installation de l'ascenseur dont elle avait apparemment un très grand besoin.

Pour célébrer son anniversaire, je lui ai acheté un gâteau « Opéra » avec ses couches moëlleuses, de crème au beurre et au café, toutes surmontées par la ganache au chocolat, et j'ai cueilli des pivoines blanches que j'ai trouvées dans le petit jardin abandonné, très évocateur d'Alphonse Mucha.

Ces jours, c'est rarement que je la rencontre, mais tous les soirs, j'attends la musique éthérée qui vient d'en haut, juste perceptible sous les vibrations interminables de l'ascenseur nouvellement installé.

Angela's home language is English.

· Day five ·

Ein verrückter Traum

Jess Nyahoe

Es war eine ganz dunkle Nacht, und ich ging die Straße hinunter. Ich sah wunderschön aus, mein langes, schwarzes Haar war halb hoch gesteckt und fiel mir über die Schulter. Ich trug einen gestickten Samtmantel über mein Seiden- und Spitzenkleid. Aber da staun ich! Was für hässliche Schuhe! Braune Clogs mit dicken Gummifersen, ein rosa Band darüber!

Auf beiden Seiten der Straße gab es Geschäfte, die geschlossen waren und es war leise, aber am Ende der Straße sah ich ein Kerzenlicht im Fenster und ging mit Eile darauf zu. Als ich die Tür aufstieß, klingelte eine kleine Glocke. Es war drinnen schwarz. Die Kerzen, die innen brannten, waren alt und fast aus. „Hallo?" sagte ich, „Ist hier jemand da?" Ich konnte die Anwesenheit einer Person fühlen.

"Certo Signora." Kam eine Stimme. Sie war tief und ich war mir nicht sicher, ob sie einem Mann oder einer Frau gehörte, aber sie waren bestimmt Italiener.

„Bitte, verkaufen Sie Schuhe?" fragte ich. Eine Pause. Meine Augen tun weh, weil sie sich in der Dunkelheit anstrengten. Plötzlich fühlte ich eine Kiste in meine Hände gelegt und ohne nachzudenken habe ich sie geöffnet. Drinnen waren zwei schwarz-rot Stiefeletten aus Schlangenleder. Ich ziehe sie an. Wie durch einen Zauber schlängelten sich die Stiefeletten an meinen Beinen hinauf! Sie haben die Farben geändert - Rot, Gelb, Rosa, Grün, Orange, Lila und Blau- der ganze Regenbogen bedeckte meine Beine bis zu meinen Schenkeln - und die Farben wechselten andauernd von schwarz-rotem Schlangenleder. Ich blieb verwundert stehen. Nach einem Moment fand ich meine Stimme und fragte "Wie viel kosten sie, bitte?"

"Niente" war die Antwort. "Stasera, sembrerai favoloso!"

Ich war spät. Der letzte Zug nach London fuhr in zehn Minuten ab. Ich rannte wie der Wind…. buchstäblich.

Die Straßen in Covent Garten waren voller Lachen und Musik. Lichter funkelten in den Bäumen, Gläser klirrten zusammen und Zigarettenrauch wirbelte zum Himmel. Ich fand die Kneipe und ging hinein. Innen war es sehr modern, was ich nicht mag. Eine Wand war vollständig aus Glas, am anderen Ende stand eine Cocktailbar mit Neon-Blitzlichtern. Tische standen hoch und glänzend schwarz, mit gleichen Stühlen. Ich ging durch unzählige Taschen und Mäntel, schiebe mich durch Menschenmassen bis ich meinen Tisch fand und setzte mich. Auf dem Tisch war ein gekochtes Hähnchen. Ich war plötzlich sehr hungrig und packte das Hähnchen. In dem Augenblick, wie die Stiefeletten, wuchs das Hähnchen in meiner Hand und sein Gesicht wandte sich meinem zu. Ich schrie und drehte mich um, um zu rennen. Ich fühlte wie sich mein Hühnerarm um sich selbst drehte und in den Kampf mit einem anderen Hähnchen verwickelt war, das an einem jungen Mann befestigt war!

Ich wachte auf. Für einen Moment starrte ich auf den Deckenventilator, der heiße Luft im Schlafzimmer herum bließ. Ich drehte mich um und umarmte meinen Verlobten Daniel.

„Alles in Ordnung, Schatz?" fragt er.

„Oh ja," antwortete ich, „nur ein wirklich verrückter Traum!"

Jess's home language is English.

Mi padre

Jonathan Ow

Me encanta escuchar música. La música es una gran parte de mi vida. Cada vez que estaba triste, escuchaba música y cada vez que estaba feliz, escuchaba música. Cada vez que lo extraño, escucho música. Cada vez que cierro mis ojos y escucho la radio en casa, me recuerda a él. Amaba su radio como si fuera su amigo. Le gustaba escuchar música de los ochenta. Su cantante favorito era Michael Bolton. Su música trajo alegría y felicidad a nuestro hogar.

Su lugar favorito era Brighton. Él solía ir allí a veces sólo por el pescado y las papas fritas con guisantes blandos. Ese era su plato favorito. Cada verano, iba a Brighton con él. Solía llevarnos allí en coche. El viaje era divertido porque él ponía su música en el coche. Me gustaba cantar en el coche con él.

Íbamos a la playa por la mañana. Le encantaba escuchar el sonido del mar. Nos sentábamos en la playa y mirábamos las olas juntos. Le gustaba leer el periódico y tomar café de un termo. A mí me gustaba relajarme al sol y mojarme los pies en el agua fría del mar.

Nuestro lugar favorito era el muelle. Íbamos allí para el almuerzo. Pedíamos pescado y papas fritas en su restaurante favorito en el muelle. Él sonreía de felicidad por la deliciosa comida. Después del almuerzo íbamos al parque de atracciones cercano. Me daba demasiado miedo montar en la montaña rusa, pero me encantaba caminar con él por el muelle y hablar con él sobre los chicos que me gustaban y cómo me volvían loco a veces. Siempre había música bonita en el muelle durante el verano y nos quedábamos a ver la puesta de sol juntos antes de volver a casa.

Este verano es diferente. He venido a Brighton por mi cuenta. Estoy sentado aquí en esta playa solo. Estoy comiendo pescado y papas fritas mientras veo la puesta de sol. Estar aquí me recuerda a él. Mi padre falleció hace cuatro años.

Lo extraño todos los días. No he estado en Brighton en tres años. Venir a Brighton este verano fue difícil para mí. Recuerdos de escuchar su música y venir a esta playa todos los veranos a comer pescado y papas fritas con él. Esto es todo lo que me queda de él. Michael Bolton estaba sonando en la radio cuando lo vi respirar su último aliento en el hospital. Con los años, escuchar música me ayudó a aceptar su muerte. La música ayudó a quitar el silencio y el vacío en casa después de su muerte.

A veces desearía que él todavía estuviera aquí conmigo. Desearía que él pudiera haber estado allí para me graduación de la universidad. Desearía que pudiera haber estado allí para verme aprender español y seguir mis sueños de trabajar como actor en el teatro. Incluso me gusta escuchar a Michael Bolton y me encanta comer pescado y papas fritas ahora. Mamá y yo lo extrañamos mucho, pero estaremos bien.

Jonathan's home language is English.

My Mummy's world

Faye Hunt

My Mummy lives in a different world,
With a virus, germs and danger.
She says I have to wash my hands,
Treat everyone like a stranger.
She uses a different language,
Words I don't understand.
`Coronavirus, social distance,
Anti-bac gel for your hands`
I can tell that she is worried,
But she tries to keep it hidden.
She waits until I've gone to bed,
Or cries when in the kitchen.

The world I live in is different,
a world that's free of care,
It's great when I wake up because
Mum and Dad are always there.
They spend time with me and play my games,
They've even replaced my teacher.
My teacher Mum is great, you know,
I hope I get to keep her!

It's hard not seeing Grandad,

but his face comes on my screen.
I hear him shout his favourite words
'Ow bin ya? Ow ya been?'
Nanny's in the background,
drinking her cup of tea.
She seems so sad lately,
I wonder what it could be.
Afternoons are best for me,
I get to learn a skill.
Last week I learnt to ride a bike,
Today I went down a hill.
I can now make lovely cupcakes,
Loads of different flavours.
I give one to Mum and one to Dad
and the rest out to my neighbours.

It's a strange world where adults live,
They are all so full of worry.
I wave and smile at my friends,
But they walk by in such a hurry.
It isn't a very happy place,
They say there's a big bad bug.
But all I really want to do
is give my family a hug.
I try to make my Mummy smile,
I give Dad a great big cuddle.
But when I go back to school
they say I'll be in a bubble.

But in the world where I live
it's one great big adventure.
I'll stay inside my bubble
and dig for buried treasure.
If I had to choose
it's my world where I'd stay.
With Mum, Dad and Alf the dog,
I'll stay and play all day.

Now the adult world is changing,
I wonder why that could be?
My parents are running round the house,
Shouting `Yippee, we're free`.

It's only been ten minutes,
But someone's at the door.
It's my Nanny and Grandad,
They couldn't wait anymore.
They give me a great big squeeze,
And say they've come to play.
It's like the world they live in,
Has finally gone away.

I told them to live in my world,
Where there's magic, fun and laughter.
They all agree to stay with us,
And live happy ever after!

Faye's home language is English – Black Country Dialect (West Midlands).

Il mercante e le sue tre figlie

hahsiarun

C'era una volta un mercante molto ricco. Aveva tre belle figlie. Le due figlie più grandi adoravano i bei vestiti e una vita confortevole, mentre la figlia più piccola era umile, simpatica, saggia e amava molto suo padre.

Un giorno il ricco mercante decise di scegliere una figlia che avrebbe preso il controllo dopo il suo pensionamento. Diede a ogni figlia un compito. Dovevano mostrargli quanto lo amavano portandogli due cose che rappresentavano il loro amore per lui. Le figlie avevano una settimana per preparare gli oggetti.

Dopo una settimana, il mercante chiamò tutte le sue figlie insieme. Chiese a ciascuna di loro di mostrargli cosa gli avevano portato.

Angela, la figlia maggiore, aveva regalato al mercante un blocco d'oro e una cassa piena di soldi. Disse: "Mio caro padre, il mio amore per te è come questo prezioso oro e denaro. Senza di loro non potremmo vivere comodamente e saremmo infelici". Il mercante fu contento di sentirlo.

La seconda figlia, Francesca, aveva regalato al mercante abiti di seta e diamanti. Disse: "Mio caro padre, il mio amore per te è come questi affascinanti abiti e gemme. Sono molto costosi e non facili da ottenere, e la nostra vita si arricchisce possedendoli". Il mercante fu contento di sentirlo.

Alla fine fu la volta della figlia minore Viola. Presentò una ciotola di sale e una ciotola di zucchero. "Mio caro padre, il mio amore per te è come questo sale e zucchero." Il mercante vide il sale e lo zucchero e si arrabbiò molto.

"Mi ami così poco? Mi deludi, figlia mia." Viola implorò suo padre di darle l'opportunità di mostrargli come si sentiva davvero. Il mercante era ancora arrabbiato, ma accettò di darle un'altra possibilità.

Più tardi il mercante e le sue figlie si sedettero insieme per cena. "Padre mio, ho cucinato per te tutti i tuoi cibi e i tuoi dolci preferiti. Per favore, prova tutti i piatti. Una volta che li hai mangiati, saprai quanto ti amo", disse Viola. Il mercante iniziò a mangiare. Dopo aver assaggiato tutti i piatti, diventò ancora più arrabbiato. "Questo è il peggior cibo che abbia mai mangiato in vita mia!" gridò.

"Esattamente, padre", disse Viola pazientemente. "Senza sale e zucchero, tutto ciò che mangiamo sarebbe insipido e noioso. Ecco come sarebbe la mia vita senza di te." Il mercante era senza parole. Alla fine si rese conto di cosa intendesse la figlia più piccola. Le due figlie più grandi si resero conto di quanto la loro sorella più giovane fosse più intelligente rispetto a loro. Promisero di imparare di più dalla loro sorella più giovane in modo da poter diventare più intelligenti. Pensarono che forse un giorno tutte e tre avrebbero potuto gestire gli affari del padre insieme.

Viola ereditò gli affari del mercante dopo il suo pensionamento. Da quel giorno, il mercante si assicurò che la cucina della sua famiglia fosse sempre piena di sale e zucchero. E vissero tutti felici e contenti.

hahsiarun's home languages are English and Malay.

La chute

Emma Hickey

« Est-ce que tu cours vite? » L'homme demanda.

« J'étais voleuse. » La fille répondit.

« Bien. Nous n'avons pas eu de voleur depuis un moment. »
Son nom était Jacques Leloup: un numéro six, sans aucun doute.
Émilie Berger n'habitait la banlieue que depuis quelques jours.
Elle n'était plus la bienvenue dans la ville. Elle n'était pas sûre si
faire de partie de la « famille » de Jacques était une bonne ou
mauvaise idée, mais c'était une vie.

En se perchant sur le bord du lit avec hésitation, elle se rendit
compte qu'elle pouvait voir la ville de sa fenêtre. L'horizon avait
l'air différent de là. À l'intérieur des murailles élevées de la ville, elle
s'était sentie protégée, mais actuellement la ville dominait l'horizon
avec sa tour de guêt blanc, menaçante. Le coucher du soleil projetait
une ombre sinistre à cause de la tour qui s'étirait vers elle, vers eux.
Une partie d'elle craignit qu'un jour la tour avancerait à toute allure
à travers le paysage pour les tuer une bonne fois pour toutes – le
monstre blanc.

Le livre en lambeaux se trouvait à côté d'elle sur le lit, le seul
livre qu'elle avait vu hormis la Bible. Quand elle était enfant, elle
avait appris les dix commandements par cœur à l'école. Six, tu ne
commettras pas de meurtre, huit, tu ne commettras pas de vol et
ainsi de suite.

Une voix à la porte la surprit.

« Il faut t'acheter de nouveaux vêtements. » C'était Jacques. Émilie tourna la tête et elle le vit, souriant alors qu'il s'adossa au chambranle.

Émilie jeta un coup d'œil à son uniforme sale qui était autrefois d'un blanc pur. Elle ramassa le livre et feuilleta les pages déchirées. En regardant la couverture du livre, blanchi au soleil, elle pouvait à peine lire le nom de l'écrivain: Boccaccio.

« Les personnages dans ce livre, ils sont comme nous. Ils se cachent d'une peste. » Émilie leva ses yeux vers Jacques et il fit oui de la tête.

« Ils ont créé leur propre Eden. À l'écart du reste du monde. Un refuge. »

« Je pensais que la ville était censée être un refuge. Un paradis, comme le Jardin d'Eden. » Émilie murmura.

Jacques soupira, en regardant par la fenêtre la silhouette des immeubles, « Je sais, mais toutes les vues du paradis ne sont pas les mêmes. Avec nous, tu es en sécurité. »

Il l'embrassa sur le front. Soudainement, Émilie cria alors qu'une douleur brûlante lui traversait la paume de la main.

Cinq… quatre… trois… deux… un. Inspirer, expirer.

« Ma main. » Émilie chuchota.

« Montre-moi. » dit-Jacques calmement.

Alors que Jacques déroulait soigneusement le bandage sur la main gauche d'Émilie, elle s'attendait à voir le pire.

« Ah, oui. » Jacques sourit: « Tu es voleuse, sans aucun doute. »

Ouvrant les yeux, elle regarda sa paume enflée et c'était comme si le « VIII » marqué dans sa peau la regardait.

Emma's home language is English.

Remnants of a life past

Sue Mayell

The spring sun rose early producing a hazy vision of mute coloured silhouetted buildings along the Bristol skyline. A faint yellowish light filled and fuzzily outlined the shapes of windows and doors in a few, but daily diminishing, number of houses, the early morning risers now favouring a lie-in. The random tempo of banging doors and revving engines has been replaced by a cacophonous mixture of bird song as if nature were rejoicing; the chirps and whistles seeming to grow louder as the world retreated behind closed doors. This was the time my husband always said, "Them's awl off t'werk then" as he brought me my first morning cuppa. One by one the residents would leave their houses and appear for a few brief moments in the street below before joining the race not to be the last to leave and go who knows where. The cars, now obsolete, sit bumper to bumper either side of the street. With sprinkles of grey dust and tinges of green moss they invoke an image of stone sarcophagi in an already desolate community.

A yellow van inches its way along the street. Its red diagonal stripes frame the much lamented government messages to stay at home and save lives. The logo no longer urges us to 'Protect the NHS', an institutional ideal of times past. The driver appears a solitary figure, he or she, it's impossible to tell, stops and exits the van. The face is completely covered, the traditional face mask now a full head covering reminiscent of a diver's wet suit and goggles. The driver leaves a box labelled 'Government Essentials' on each doorstep, a bi-weekly ritual and another new government initiative.

My delivery is collected by my care assistant who ensures everything is sterilised and ready for my use. Today is my 100th birthday and as I sit looking out of the window, I check the clock. It will soon be time for my remote media link-up with the other residents who will sing me 'Happy Birthday'.

It is years since I moved out of my home and into Fairlawns Care Centre. When my husband died, I didn't want to live alone. The view from my window is a contradiction of memories; the same buildings and streets, but now dirty and unkempt and silently devoid of human life. The few remaining neighbours are older but invisible. No one goes out anymore, there are no "gud marnin" greetings exchanged today or any other, not since this new virus strain. Human contact outside of households is strictly forbidden. My only personal contact is the twice-daily visits from my faceless carer inside her protective suit. Life since lockdown has changed immeasurably. I sit quietly, as I have every morning for many years and wait.

Sue's home language is English.

While there's life, there's hope

Jasmine Buchner

With my cup of coffee, I make myself at home on my balcony in London on this sunny summer day. The sun rays dance on my face while the coffee aroma gently wafts around my nose. That feeling of ease will change as soon as I go out into the street. The fear then wraps around me like a coat haunting me all the way outside. Back home, I will hide again behind my locked door. Taking off my face mask, this is the place I feel most alive right now.

We are now living in times of fear, but also of humility, resistance and hope. In times of pandemic, it's not possible to give live concerts with classical music. This makes my colleagues and me more than depressed. Of course, there is digital transmission. But to embrace the art of music, you have to experience it with a live orchestra. Unemployment, especially for us artists, is more than just a threat to our existence. Sometimes I wake up at night plagued by nightmares that haunt me like a monster through the gloom.

But after a few days, I have realised that I can change something about the situation. At least in terms of mindset. Maybe I can see Covid-19 not as a threat, but as an opportunity. Perhaps the media is too panicky, which can influence you so much that you suffer from emotional paralysis. To a certain extent, we allow ourselves to be manipulated by others. We have not given much thought to what positive things can come out of the situation. My musician colleague Cindy, who called me a few days ago, also appeared to be emotionally trapped by the lack of perspective. Her words spoke their own language.

'Sarah, this whole situation will end badly if we all let it affect us without taking action ourselves.' I could feel her anxiety in every single word.

'Maybe we should think of something to help us get through this challenging period. Encouraging other people not to be alone should be our goal.'

'That sounds exciting. What'd you have in mind?'

'I was talking to Bruno our Italian pianist recently, and he told me about a new Decameron project based on the work of the medieval writer Boccaccio. The idea is to celebrate hope and perhaps we could take this as an example by giving the people in our neighbourhood free concerts.'

Cindy was enthusiastic.

'What a wonderful idea. I'll talk to the conservatoire. We could perform there while the neighbours could listen at home.'

Twelve hours later we knew we could give our neighbours a wonderful time full of music and hope for the future.

Jasmine's home language is German.

Un bijoux précieux

Sarah Evans

Il y a longtemps, c'était la tradition dans un village pour tout le monde de passer leur temps libre à chercher un bijou précieux. La tradition a commencé quand un ancien voyant du village a trouvé un manuscrit ancien.

Although it had a small piece missing, the manuscript was considered to be sacred and was placed inside an ornate gold frame in the town hall. In spite of the damage, it was still possible to read the handwritten words, 'When you discover a precious jewel, all your problems will be over.'

Many stories were passed down about how the precious jewels would change your life if only you could find one. They could light up the sky, cure the sick and give the finder endless riches. Before breakfast, after work, the villagers would hardly speak to each other, they were so engrossed in their searching. Every day, every week, every month, every year the villagers searched but the precious jewels remained elusive.

One day a young girl from the village felt sad. « Mère, nous ne faisons jamais rien d'autre que de chercher ce bijou. Il y a d'autres chose dans la vie! »

« Quand nous découvrirons un bijou précieux, tous nos problèmes seront terminés ».

« Nous ne découvrirons jamais un bijou précieux! » The little girl shouted angrily and ran out of the house.

She ran and ran, over hills and through valleys, to a place she had never been before. After a while, a delicate flashing light in the distance caught her eye. Un bijou précieux? As she got closer she realised it was just a glistening stone. However her eyes were drawn to the ground around the stone which had been disturbed. Frantically digging, she found a metal box. She wrenched open the lid with such force that it flew a great distance away, crashing to the ground.

However it was what was inside that grabbed her attention. A tiny scrap of paper with two words written on it. « Vous êtes » Vous êtes? Qu'est-ce que cela signifie? She repeated the phrase to herself as she looked at the piece of paper. It looked very old, and it looked familiar. Wow! She thought. It was like the piece of the ancient manuscript that was in the town hall. It was the missing piece! So the complete message actually reads « Quand vous découvrirez que vous êtes un bijou précieux, tous nos problèmes seront terminés. » Elated, she ran home to tell her mother the good news that they didn't have to search anymore.

« Mère! J'ai trouvé le manuscrit. Je sais que nous sommes les précieux bijoux ».

« Je n'ai pas le temps pour les jeux ». The little girl felt sad again. She showed the missing piece of the manuscript to others in the village but always got the same response. Over time she came to realise they were not ready for the truth. However she got comfort in her new found freedom from searching and she glowed with an inner happiness knowing that *they* were the real precious jewels.

Sarah's home language is English.

El fondo del cup

Luke Denbeigh-Griffiths

La puerta se cerró behind me con un click and I found myself otra vez más en el forecourt. La entrevista concluded solo moments before, front and centre in my mind. I reached dentro de mi pocket en busca del móvil, and strode por el parking back out into suburbia. Los pantalones—tight polyester, sweaty en el muggy weather. I wrenched my hand free. Looking down, el móvil estaba allí, una tostada en el kitchen floor, boca abajo on the pavement. Sighing, me resigné al cracked screen inevitable. ¡Qué se joda Samsung!

Pasando por las gates giré instintivamente to the right y me paré. Which way had I come? I would have googleado mi ubicación, pero la pantalla estaba too far gone. I might have vuelto al edificio to ask for directions, pero no quería undermine la buena impresión que había dado en la entrevista. Así que, I stuck al instinto inicial and looked out hopefully for passersby to venir a mi ayuda.

Las casas aquí were indistinguishable entre sí—a string of sausages, a line of numbered boxes in a warehouse. Me imaginé living in one of them. Coming home at the end of la jornada laboral to my chica, and dinner in front of un sitcom estadounidense. The mediocre life that loomed. Pero una vida cómoda como un par de zapacasas viejas.

I dreamt of escaping esta vida, of catching el primer tren a cualquier sitio y empezar de nuevo. Soñaba de fleeing al mediterráneo, barefoot on the arena dorada, breeze in my hair. I was young en un mundo de posibilidades, "the world is your lobster", como dijo mi tía una vez.

A pesar de eso, me sentía gripped por el miedo, it held me a este sitio, it held me a esta mujer, a esta vida.

The street curved to the left y continué on through the sprawling monotony—passing casas, sleepers beneath a train. Click, click, click. Not a soul to be seen.

Eventually, me encontré con un retail park, and ready for some refreshment, entré. El super had a cafe, así que pedí my café solo de siempre and sat down a reflexionar sobre la vida. My eyes flitted de una foto ampliada de modelos con sus hollywood smiles, a los sachets de UHT milk, y la surly young cafe assistant, and finalmente my eyes se detuvieron sobre the black millpond del café. I stared into it, into myself. Mis problemas, azúcar no disuelta, sat in ambush for me to finish. Necesitaba enfrentarme a estos problemas, a pre-emptive assault contra mis demonios. Cogí el little plastic stirrer and probed el fondo del cup.

It wasn't el miedo a la muerte, it was el temor a la soledad that really got me, y el fear of taking risks. Me encontraba en este safe harbour, el alma atormentada por el urge to break free.

Tomé un sip, and told myself, al terminar el café I will decide... si quedarme or go.

Luke's home language is English.

The journey

Patrick Lau Ka Chung

Tyler is a 16-year-old high school student who lives in Hong Kong. He is also a dreamer and a language enthusiast but he is always too shy to seize the opportunity to fulfil his language related dream. He wanted to become a translator, an English teacher and even wanted to meet friends from all over the world.

One day the opportunity presented itself to Tyler - there was an exchange programme to Singapore (10 days) for those who were the top 10 in the final year English exam. Tyler is one of them.

Although Tyler has some talents in language learning, he can't speak in front of foreigners because he is afraid that those native speakers will judge him and laugh at him when he speaks. This fear overwhelmed him during the first part of the trip; he didn't say much and relied instead on the other students speaking for him.

On the sixth day, things changed. There were 10 other students from the Singapore side, and Tyler was forced to interact with Henry for the remaining days. Henry is the exact opposite of Tyler: he is fearless, talkative and very energetic. In the remaining days, they have to stick together and perform some tasks or activities prepared by the organizers. One of the activities is called 'Treasure Hunt', where the participants need to find the treasure with clues written in both Chinese and English. Tyler thinks Henry also can finish this activity by himself with his 'unlimited energy' but Henry has a huge weakness since he is not good with Chinese words and stumbles on Chinese riddles. '有面没有口，有脚没有手，虽有四只脚，自己不会走（猜一家具）' (It has a face but no mouth, it has feet but no hands. Though it has four feet, it can't walk by itself. Guess: a furniture). Henry starts to panic but Tyler uses his talent and solves the riddle 'The answer is a table!' They have each other's back, solve all the riddles along the way and get the treasure in the fastest time. From that point on, Henry asked Tyler to teach him Chinese and in order to do that Tyler needs to use English as a medium to teach him about Chinese. Even though Henry's Mandarin pronunciation is not good, he is not afraid to speak in front of Tyler, when he is asked the reason why, he replied 'Practice makes perfect, if you can't speak the language enough, you will never learn anything from it.' After some time, Tyler is no longer afraid to speak in front of native speakers or fluent speakers. What Henry said helped him a lot.

After the journey, Tyler went back to Hong Kong and participated in different English public speaking competitions. Although he didn't win any of them, he liked the feeling of speaking English in front of a big audience.

Patrick's home language is Cantonese.

Une évasion audacieuse

Samatha Rodgers

Le 15 juin 1940 et, en à peine une décennie, Montparnasse dans le
14e arrondissement de Paris était passée d'une capitale culturelle
animée à une ville fantôme sans vie. Les années folles étaient
désormais révolues.

Hélène, 19 ans, originaire de Montparnasse, avait rencontré
Joseph, 18 ans, un garçon de parents anglais vivant à Paris, à peine
sept mois plus tôt. Ils ne sont pas partis avec leurs familles deux
jours avant, en partie parce qu'ils étaient enlacés dans la corde
suffocante du jeune amour, qui s'enroulait autour d'eux comme du
lierre autour d'un tronc d'arbre et, en partie, parce que Joseph avait
voulu se battre avec la Résistance. Cependant, en l'espace d'une
journée, tout avait changé.

« Joseph! », Hélène s'exclama depuis la salle de bain de la maison
ce matin-là, « je pense que je suis enceinte ».

« Grab your things, we need to get you to your family. Food's
already scarce and we can't risk the Nazis discovering that you're
carrying an English child. They'll send us to a prison camp », Joseph
cria avec inquiétude.

Il comprenait parfaitement le français mais le parlait trop
lentement, il parlait donc anglais.

Ils ont attendu 22.30 h. Aussi silencieux que des souris essayant
de s'échapper de la chouette rôdante, ils chargèrent prudemment

mais précipitamment la voiture avec leurs deux valises, remplies uniquement du strict nécessaire.

Les crêperies et les cafés autrefois accueillants étaient maintenant complètement vides et les regardaient avec suspicion alors qu'ils rampaient dans la voiture après le couvre-feu.

Sous le ciel noircissant, ils partirent.

Exacerbé, Joseph murmura, « we can't go back ».

« Je sais », dit Hélène en sanglots.

Ils avancèrent à vitesse réduite à l'approche de l'Avenue du Maine, pas de phares, pas de moteur qui hurle. Joseph hésita et commença à trembler physiquement, son pied gauche tapa sur l'embrayage comme un tambour. Hélène caressa l'épaule de Joseph de manière rassurante.

« Ça va? », demanda-t-elle.

« We're going to be exposed on this road, I don't know if we'll make it »

« Reste optimiste », elle exhorta.

Le black-out fonctionnait jusqu'à présent en leur faveur. Étonnamment, bien que des camions nazis aient bordé les rues, ils étaient vides, mais suffisamment intimidants pour envoyer un message clair que leurs occupants étaient partout.

Désormais sous contrôle nazi, Paris commençait déjà à perdre son identité. Des drapeaux nazis triomphants étaient déjà fièrement suspendus au château de Versailles et sur la tour Eiffel et la ville fonctionnait maintenant à l'heure allemande. Ils ont dépassé un Soldatenheim et un Soldatenkaffee qui, il y a quelques jours seulement, étaient des hôtels populaires.

Soudain, à la station de métro Alesia, ils furent accueillis par une attaque aveuglante de lampes de poche.

Ils s'arrêtèrent. Un homme en uniforme s'avança vers la voiture.

« Zeig mir deine Papiere », il ordonna.

Puis, ils entendirent des coups de feu, suivi de voix françaises.

Etait-ce la résistance qui se cachait?

Samantha's home language is English.

Jinxed love

Marcin Andrzej Lukasik

Crowded with poisonous snakes, deadly reptiles and feared human-eating shamans, the jungle seemed the safest shelter for the master thief wanted by the revengeful Sultan's hordes. Having escaped the killers, Sudrajat - a handsome young man - arrived in infamous Hutan Ular, the snake jungle in Sunda Kingdom. He was admired by some and wanted by many. Only one thought was keeping him strong: the beauty of the Sultan's only daughter, Dewi Ratna. The last words she said to him were: 'Tolong, kembali lagi...' – 'Please come back...'. His raison d'être was to get back to the woman he loved. His heart was filled with desire and his senses were left to starve.

After months and tens of snake bites, Sudrajat left for the Sultan's residence. The ruler employed thousands of servants and kept dozens of lions, lizards and elephants at his home. Days passed and the traveller was nearing his destination. On one foggy, chilly day, an enormous raven flew out of a forest and tried to attack Sudrajat. He killed the bird but a woman wearing a round hat approached out of nowhere and screamed: 'Kamu tidak akan mencintai lagi!' In revenge for killing her beloved bird, the witch cursed Sudrajat and said he would never love again.

Entering the royal residence seemed impossible but Sudrajat, a gifted storyteller, managed to pass the guards. He hid in the cellar and now he was closer to the princess than ever before. He could see a corridor with heavy brass doors in its end that could lead him to the arms of his love. In autumn, when the air was steamy and wet, his chance rose - the Sultan left to suppress a minor rebellion and the princess was left lightly guarded.

That was the chance Sudrajat sought. He bribed the nightwatchman and gained access to her chamber. The dreamer had one leg in heaven. The princess was sitting on her gold chair. He shouted: 'Ini aku. Aku kembali.' – 'It's me, I'm back' but Dewi Ratna replied nothing. All he heard was a raven squawk.

He got closer. Close enough to see Dewi's face and what he saw shook him to the core. Her face was pale like coconut flesh and her palms were cold like a mountain river. His princess was fatally poisoned. His heart slowed down and his hope perished. The mission failed and the witch's wicked words were fulfilled. Sudrajat screamed in pain and his voice was heard miles away.

Guards entered the room and left him in a pool of blood. Sudrajat was denounced as the killer of the princess and his corpse was fed to the ravens.

Marcin's home language is Polish.

· Day six ·

The breakfast

Emer Fahy

The cat edged along the poolside, the skin of the bald patches in its fur showing pinkish grey. Niamh watched Janet, spotting the animal as she emerged from her room, make a beeline for it (don't touch it) then stoop to pat its bony back.

'They really should do something about that animal' said Janet, sitting down. 'I doubt it's the hotel's cat. It'll be a stray' Niamh answered, taking hand sanitiser from the pocket of her cargo pants and handing it to her.

'Anyone know what we're doing today?' asked Frank, his bald head already perspiring in the morning's rising heat, his bushwhackers hat on the table beside him. 'Cultural outing to see the lion in the zoo next door, I believe. Hear him roaring last night?' said Malcolm. 'Don't mind him, Janet' interjected his wife, Sandra, as Janet looked up, outraged. 'He's only teasing you'.

'We are,' Kathy paused as she consulted the trip notes on her iPhone, 'taking the scenic bus route to Portoviejo to see the colourful street market then visiting a pottery employing disabled young people'. 'Better get your wallet out this time, Janet, and buy some wonky mugs' grinned Malcolm.

As the last of the group appeared, the waiter came to take their breakfast orders. *Pan con queso, huevos, fruta, jugo de naranja, café*....

'I'm worried about that cat' said Janet again. 'Niamh, you speak Spanish. Come with me to Reception and ask them to take it to a vet.' Niamh hesitated. She wasn't confident in Spanish, though was frequently told you couldn't tell her nationality when she spoke it. No Galway accent coming through her *castellano* even though it had survived thirty years in London intact. She doubted their request would be welcome but she did owe Janet for gamely taking to the salsa floor with her the previous night, to awkwardly shake their Northern European hips.

Lucía saw the two hotel guests, from the first tour group in months, approaching. The tall one in front, both scruffy in their expensive breathable fabrics. She smoothed her skirt and smiled brightly.

'*Buenos días*' the shorter one began, in Spanish of unknown origin. '*Mi compañera ama a los animales*'. A pause. '*Um, es inglesa*' the woman added, by way of further explanation. '*Piensa que el gato necesita un veterinario.*' Lucía, still smiling, '*No es nuestro gato, señora*', whilst thinking *maldito bruto*. Another pause then the guest, pleading, '*Lo comprendo, pero…*'. They both glanced at the intense, determined looking *compañera* who barked 'Well, will they?' Lucía capitulated. '*Haré una llamada*'.

As the guests returned to their table, she picked up the phone and found the number on speed dial. '*Dígame*' growled the voice at the other end. Lucía imagined Juan, shirt sleeves pushed up over arms as furry as the animals he loved and looked after. '*Tengo otro para ti*'.

The roar of lions drifted over the enclosure. Those far from their native shore waited for breakfast. *Pan con queso, huevos, fruta, jugo de naranja, café….*

Emer's home language is English.

Die Verhaftung

Bob McGonigle

Der Hase Wachtmeister still stand mit Pistole in der Hand.
Seine Uniform - rote Mütze dekoriert mit goldenem Band,
gegen kalten Wind und Schnee, einen langen blauen Pelzmantel,
und, gefüttert mit Lammwolle, schwere schwarze Stiefel.

Nüsse tragend, vor Kälte zittert die kleine braune Maus,
nicht weit von der Begrüßungstür ihres warmen Hauses.
Der Hase Wachtmeister stand zwischen ihr und der Tür,
und blickte auf das Diebesgut, gestohlen aus Wald und Flur.

Der Polizist dachte an die Familie Maus,
hungrig in ihrem kleinen feuchten Haus.
Schnee bedeckte die Welt, die Luft war bitterkalt.
Der Polizist machte kehrt und ging zurück in den Wald.

Bob's home language is English.

Une célébration de la diversité

Kashain Arshad

Pour moi, je pense que dans ce monde les différences sont sous-estimées. L'inégalité peut exister. Cependant, les différences doivent être célébrées.

Pendant mes années scolaires, j'ai été victime d'intimidation parce que je suis musulman. Mais, cette histoire n'a pas l'intention de s'attarder sur ces années. J'ai l'intention de célébrer un monde différent avec un récit sur la diversité.

La diversité, pour moi, est ce qui rend notre monde particulier. J'ai la double nationalité. Je suis écossais et pakistanais. Ma langue maternelle est l'anglais et j'étudie le français. Ma femme a la double nationalité. Elle est galloise et pakistanaise. Elle est bilingue, anglais et ourdou. J'ai des amis qui viennent d'horizons différents avec des goûts différents pour la musique, le cinéma et la politique mais nous célébrons ces différences.

Dans le climat actuel, nous nous soutenons mutuellement parce que nos différences sont ce qui rend le monde plus fort. L'Écosse est un pays où nous accueillons ouvertement tout le monde et j'ai l'intention d'écrire sur ce sujet.

Mon père est arrivé en Écosse en 1977 sans argent. Il vivait avec mon oncle et il travaillait dans son magasin où il a rencontré ma mère. Ils se sont mariés peu de temps après. Mais le racisme est arrivé après le mariage. Ils entendaient des racistes dire « Retournez dans votre propre pays Paki ».

Toutefois, mon père n'a jamais laissé ces insultes l'atteindre et a plutôt aidé ses voisins en faisant leurs courses ou en leur prêtant de l'argent si nécessaire.

Quand j'ai demandé pourquoi il avait aidé les racistes, il a répondu que les gens avaient peur car les médias dépeignent les immigrés d'une manière négative et que la seule façon de changer leur état d'esprit était d'être bienveillant à leur égard.

Lentement, les opinions des gens ont commencé à changer et ils sont devenus amis avec mon père et la communauté musulmane.

Donc, à mon avis, une personne n'est pas née raciste, elle est le résultat de préjugés négatifs.

Par conséquent, un monde différent devrait être célébré. Nous avons tous des races, des religions et des langues différentes mais ces différences sont ce qui nous rendent uniques dans la société.

Kashain's home language is English.

L'amore ai tempi del Covid

Julia Milne

Durante il periodo del lockdown, quattro studenti condividono una soffitta a Greenwich. Mark, il pittore, sta dipingendo un paesaggio del Tamigi e Colin, che studia filosofia, sta riflettendo sulla vita. Ricardo studia medicina. È spagnolo e sta tentando di scrivere un articolo in inglese che trova difficile, e quindi c'è carta sparsa su tutto il pavimento. Sono tutti tristi, i soldi mancano quasi sempre, ma soprattutto di questi tempi. Tuttavia, Sebastian, che suona il violino, torna a casa euforico dopo aver trascorso la giornata a suonare per strada per le persone in coda al supermercato. Ha dei soldi, e porta a casa molte lattine di birra.

I quattro amici decidono di festeggiare, quando inaspettatamente giunge Brian. Brian è il padrone di casa che ha appena staccato l'elettricità ed ora chiede l'affitto. Gli studenti lo implorano a lungo, lo riempiono di birra, e lo portano al parco per continuare i loro festeggiamenti.

Ricardo, che non beve mai molto, si attarda a finire il suo articolo. Il suo articolo è importante. In realtà, l'opinione di Ricardo dissente da quella della maggioranza. Crede che la paura del virus sia più pericolosa che la malattia stessa e sente il desiderio di incitare le persone a mangiare sano e a fare passeggiate immersi nella natura.

Si sta facendo buio e Ricardo sta cercando i fiammiferi per accendere una candela, quando sente bussare alla porta. È la sua vicina che è uscita con l'immondizia ed accidentalmente si è chiusa fuori dal suo appartamento. Lei è poco vestita e deve telefonare a un fabbro. Ricardo la fa entrare e poi fruga freneticamente tra i piatti sporchi, bozze e biancheria per trovare il suo telefonino. Lei lo aiuta e, quando la mano di Ricardo incontra la sua, Ricardo la guarda per un momento nel chiaro di luna. È veramente bella, giovane e dolce; oltretutto, sta tremando di freddo, ha la fronte che le scotta e una tosse persistente. Ricardo la avvolge nel cappotto vecchio di Colin e le dà un caldo abbraccio. Dopo aver trovato il suo telefonino, lo nasconde in una tasca perché vuole passare un po' più di tempo con Mimì per conoscerla meglio. I due parlano delle loro vite e lui scopre che lei studia moda. È amore a prima vista. Tuttavia, Mimì è malata, forse ha il virus. Dovrebbero andare in isolamento per almeno due settimane. Che sogno meraviglioso! L'intimità viene interrotta dalle grida ubriache degli amici di Ricardo. Dalla finestra e ad alta voce, Ricardo spiega ai suoi amici che ha improvvisamente contratto il virus, e che quindi dovrà isolarsi immediatamente.

In questo momento, Ricardo vede l'amore ovunque. Vede i suoi amici preoccupati per lui. Vede che Brian offre loro un posto dove stare. Vede Mark e Musetta, la sua ex-fidanzata, abbracciarsi. La felicità di Ricardo si irradia nell'universo. Sa che Mimì si riprenderà e che il suo articolo sarà un sincero appello al mondo per svegliarsi. Questo è un contagio nel senso più bello.

Julia's home language is English.

A world away

F.A. Hershey

The countdown to Helena's trip of a lifetime had started, and there were only a couple of weeks to go. The whole family couldn't contain their frantic excitement that had spread fast, reaching far and wide within their small rural Brazilian community. The frenzied atmosphere mingled with Helena's edginess at the enormity of what was about to happen on the cusp of her womanhood. This was to be a life-changing journey to the other side of the Atlantic Ocean, to a faraway country where everything was the opposite of what was known and familiar to Helena.

Grandma Mary was proud of her granddaughter's courage to spread her wings and fly the coop but she was also half worried to see Helena go. The myriad of aunts and uncles had expressed extreme opposites about this trip – some were delighted and wished they were the ones going instead, but others were less open to this sudden change in the order of things.

Great Granny Nena – aka Vó Nena – had been the quietest of them all amongst the usually agitated family chatter. She was also the person Helena most cared about; Helena avoided thoughts of saying goodbye to this woman who had brought her up, the matriarch of the family who had never left her home town in her lifetime, the woman who was almost a centenarian, with piercing blue eyes that sparkled with wisdom.

When the family talked about the language people spoke in that country called England, their culture, their food, the long and arduous history, the architecture, the underground train, the museums and the cold weather, Nena listened carefully, but she never joined in.

The day before the trip Helena went to Nena's room. It had always been easy and natural to talk to Nena, but this time Helena had to focus on controlling her emotions to keep the tears at bay and mostly nodded and smiled, as Nena offered her guidance.

Nena never had much in the way of financial stability during her long life. Nevertheless, her generosity reached beyond the bounds of material possession and she had a completely different sense of what could be considered excessive in the way of spending. The tears spilled, however, when Nena offered Helena a R$10 note – which did not buy much more than a few sweets - so that she could purchase some snacks on the way. She didn't want Helena to go hungry because the journey would be so long. Years later, Helena still held that note as a souvenir from an era that would never come back. She could never spend it.

Nena reminded Helena not to forget her values behind, never mind her "valuables" and that she should never forget where she came from. *'Vou sentir muitas saudades de voce viu!'* Nena had said. That word *saudades* - like a sad longing for someone - had hung in the air then and especially now that Nena was no longer here. That bitter sweet yearning would never go away.

F.A. Hershey's home language is Portuguese.

Un mundo de sueños

Gusthegecko

Paso mucho tiempo soñando despierto. Sueño con un mundo donde soy libre. Libre para vagar, aventurarse y explorar. Libre para sentir el sol en el suelo y calentar la arena entre mis dedos. Libre para amar y ser amado. Libre para perseguir mis sueños. Libre de discriminación. Libre de juicio. Libre de depredadores. Libre para solo… ser. Sueño con comida fresca y agua potable fría y limpia. Sueño con piscinas tibias para empapar mi piel seca. Sueño en tomar la mano de mi madre en enfermedad y salud.
Sueño con un mundo donde todos sean iguales;
no importa el sexo, la raza o el tamaño;
no importa si es humano o animal.
Sueño con un mundo donde
«amar a tu prójimo»
es más que un mandamiento.
Donde estoy a salvo. Donde soy suficiente.
Donde se escucha mi voz. Donde vivimos en paz.
Pero solo soy un lagarto
que vive en cautiverio,
donde mis sueños están
fuera de este mundo.

The author's home language is English.

Gated community

Amiee Welbourn

I had never stepped foot outside of the city walls - only a few had - and they'd never returned to tell us what it was like. There were rumours, of course, about a dangerous beast that lived in the shadow of the trees. As a child, I loved to feel the warmth of the sun by reaching through the iron gates that my arms were just thin enough to squeeze through. I'd soon be yanked back by a guard who turned red in the face whilst screaming at me.

Everything will change after tonight. I had barely begun to grieve my mother's passing before realising all she had left me was her abusive, drunkard of a husband, my father, who demanded respect without showing any himself. It was terrifying, waiting until he passed out, to pack a bag. I couldn't risk spending even one night alone with him.

I started walking to Sasha's house. Her father was the governor and, although he didn't approve, she would sneak food out to us when mother was too sick to prepare meals. Sasha's family was one of the only ones who were fed properly. Most of us looked very similar with our pale skin, dark hair and gaunt, malnourished bodies. I would also sleep on her balcony when the monster would appear behind my father's eyes.

The city streets may as well have been underground. Homes had been built on top of homes to accommodate a growing population in an area of land without any chance of expansion, blocking out any natural light. Only the top-most dwellings would see the sun daily.

Arriving at Sasha's, I plead with her to come with me.

'I can't, it's suicide!' She furiously whispers. It was always a risk coming here, her father could catch us at any time, and he would force me to go back to my home. Whether or not he would put me in the stocks for being out after dark would be another matter.

'What if it isn't? What if we could be happy away from here?' I beg. She's too scared though. I hold her for what seems like forever, my only friend who had helped feed me and keep me safe. I can't even muster the words to say goodbye. She kisses my forehead and turns back to her bedroom.

I dodge the guards by keeping to the alleys and staying as silent as possible. I climb a post that leads to a balcony where I jump to the top of the wall.

I hear a clatter, glass breaking, and a scream. I'm frozen, perched on the wall. A guard's radio creates a crackling sound and I listen closely.

'It's the governor's house, there's been a break-in.' Heavy footsteps indicate they are running from somewhere nearby towards the commotion. I breathe again when they are far enough away.

Sasha's still protecting me, even when I'm abandoning her.

I take one last glance at the city, before leaping off the wall.

Amiee's home language is English.

Global

Claire Leather

L'histoire que je vous raconte décrit un temps perdu. C'était le temps des rues désertées, écoles silencieuses et la liberté enterrée depuis longtemps. Je me souviens de ce temps. C'était un monde si délirant qu'aujourd'hui tout le monde l'a oublié. Venez visiter ce monde avec moi- au nom de la mémoire.

"您要什么？" la femme qui travaillait au marché a demandé. "要两个小鸡。我的妈妈身体不好。她必须吃鸡汤。" C'était un vieil homme qui parlait, d'un air inquiet. "现在很多人不太好。" La marchande a répondu crûment. "对。 她发烧，她嗓子有一点儿发炎。她咳嗽很多很多！" 老人说。"她吃药了吗？" "吃了。她吃了中药，也吃了西药。身体还不好。她必须看医生！" C'est à ce moment que deux hommes sont arrivés et ont regardé les produits soigneusement. Qu'est-ce qu'ils cherchaient? "找什么？" La marchande a demandé, curieuse. 'Wir möchten chinesische Medizin für seinen Husten. Haben Sie etwas, bitte?' a dit l'un des hommes. "我英文说得不好！说汉语吧！" A-t-elle dit, embarrassée. Enfin l'homme a réussi à acheter le médicament chinois. 'Henning, du musst diese Medizin schlucken,' a insisté le mec blond à son ami, 'und du nimmst auch zwei Schmerztabletten. Du musst schnell zum Flughafen fahren. Es ist sehr spät und dein Flug wird bald starten!' L'homme était triste de partir de Chine, mais au même temps il était très content car bientôt il allait travailler dans une station de ski en Italie! Welcome on board BA 3456 flight from Beijing to Milan, l'hôtesse de l'air a dit. 'We hope you have a pleasant flight.' À bord de l'avion, il y avait beaucoup de nationalités différentes – Chinois, Français, Anglais, Allemands et, bien sûr, Italiens. Un véritable mélange - tous étaient assis côte-à-côte dans la cabine. En arrivant à Milan, l'Allemand avait la tête qui tournait, et toute la neige des Alpes ne réduisait ni sa fièvre ni son frisson. Aussitôt qu'il est arrivé au chalet, il s'est écroulé sur le lit, épuisé. ¿Tienes sed? a demandé un moniteur de ski espagnol, et pendant la nuit, l'Espagnol a cherché plusieurs verres d'eau pour étancher la soif de l'Allemand. 'Danke schön Señor', a dit l'Allemand le matin suivant, 'Heute soll ich zu Hause bleiben um gesund zu werden. Ich fühle mich schlecht'. Dans les jours qui suivirent, l'Espagnol a annoncé son retour en Espagne. Quiero volver directamente a mi casa en Barcelona. Aux dires de tous, un virus mortel originaire d'un marché chinois était en train de se propager à travers le monde– et personne n'était immunisé. Le monde s'est rétracté. Tout le monde est resté chez soi. Le silence, le vide et la peur ont dominé. C'était un temps surréel, et un temps qui est de nos jours perdu.

Claire's home language is English.

High tide

Julie Johnson

The girl is walking along the beach, her toes sink into the wrinkled sand. 'Why go to the seaside, then stay at the cafe?' she asks herself. She looks back at the sea wall; her parents are sitting outside a French cafe with their glasses of wine, but she can't see them from here. Reassured that she is safely out of sight, she dances along the edge of the water, practising her French words as she hops in and out of the gentle waves.

'Le sable, la mer, l'eau.' She scrutinises the grey water, 'Il n'y a pas de poisson.' Green ropes of seaweed wind around her ankles and she kicks them away, back into the deeper water. 'What is the word for seaweed? L'herbe mauvaise de la mer?'

She hasn't noticed that the beach is empty, all the other people have disappeared and the sand is covered in water. Waves reach up to the sea wall, which looks much further away than she remembers it.

Some parts of the beach are sandy but there are clusters of slippery rocks which are now covered by water. She starts to inch her way back to the sea wall. 'Non, non!' she hears from the promenade and a Frenchman waves her away from her path. The water swirls back briefly, revealing glistening rocks, then a wave rushes in hiding the danger. She is starting to feel frightened and worried as her parents haven't noticed yet that she is missing.

'Help, help me,' she mutters under her breath, too scared to shout out loud, as this will be admitting she has a problem. It can't be that serious, the water is still below her knees although each time a wave comes in, it splashes higher, catching her arms, her chest.

Her foot slides on a stone; it wobbles but her other foot has found the sand and cautiously she moves in that direction. As she gets closer to the sea wall she sees the watching crowd. A man stretches out a hand to pull her up the steep slope.

'Respire, respire,' he says as she gasps and staggers onto the safety of the promenade. She wants to say thank you, she has the word 'merci' ready in her mouth, but she is still gasping from her ordeal.

She escapes from her rescuers and joins her parents silently at their table. They don't need to know what happened as she is safe now. 'Would you like an ice-cream?' her mother asks as if nothing has happened. The girl shakes her head, she is ready with her words now. 'Un chocolat chaud, s'il vous plait.'

Julie's home language is English.

Vide de sens

Ouafâ Mhaoui

Labas 3lik ya bladi, labas 3likoum ya wladi.
Li mrid allah ychfi, ou li d3if allah y9owi.
ou li b3id allah yrado lwlado yafar7o bi.
Ou n9olik ma3andk char, al7amdoulah ra73lik dar.
Mhmeken ljar7 kbir, keyn rabbi fo9 akbar.

J'espère que tu vas bien, mon pays, j'espère que vous allez bien mes enfants.
Que Dieu guérisse les malades et rende les faibles forts.
Et que Dieu renvoie ceux qui sont loin à leurs enfants pour qu'ils soient
heureux avec eux.
Et vous dise que tout va bien, votre douleur est guérie.
Peut-être que ta blessure est trop grosse, mais aie la foi parce qu'il y a
encore un dieu au-dessus, qui est le plus grand.

Paroles par Yahya Tabich, traduites par Ouafâ Mhaoui.

Les paroles de cette chanson lui rappellent ce que ses parents
disaient en famille; elle se sent en sécurité en les entendant encore et
encore. Ça se reproduit, elle le sent. Luttant pour ouvrir les yeux et
submergée par le sentiment que tout n'est pas normal. Elle
commence sa journée en descendant les escaliers, en entrant dans la
pièce où sa famille prend le déjeuner, avec les rires bruyants et les
disputes de ses parents, en sécurité chez elle. Niya ne peut imaginer

vivre sans eux. Elle aime son héritage et tout ce qu'elle est en tant qu'individu et membre de sa famille. Brusquement, tout se termine et chaque membre de sa famille disparaît, s'évapore dans l'air, la laissant debout au milieu d'un salon vide.

Un beau rayon de lumière brille à travers ses paupières et ne semble pas la réveiller ; ses beaux grands yeux encore fermés, elle attend la sonnerie matinale de son réveil. Mais elle se réveille trempée de sueur et réalise qu'elle a fait le même rêve qu'elle fait chaque nuit. La plus grande peur de Niya est devenue réalité il y a six mois lorsqu'elle a perdu ses parents. Depuis, elle fait ce rêve où tout redevient normal ; ses parents sont toujours vivants et la couvrent d'amour, un amour que personne ne peut égaler.

On s'attend à une journée chaude et ensoleillée, mais ce sera une journée chaude et ensoleillée assez différente. Tout ce à quoi elle était habituée, sa routine, ses collègues, ses amis, sa famille, ont disparu en un battement de paupières. C'est calme dehors et personne ne se précipite où que ce soit. Restant immobile, elle se demande ce qui a changé? Personne ne sait vraiment ce qui s'est exactement passé, seulement que le monde entier s'est immobilisé. Pas de travail, pas d'école, pas de festivals, pas d'activités amusantes, pas de visites aléatoires. Tout le monde est limité à son domicile et ne peut sortir que pour les urgences et les courses à l'épicerie. Dehors, on tue les gens sans merci, en particulier les personnes âgées. Niya se sent coupable, parce qu'elle a toujours souhaité que le monde s'arrête juste une minute. Une minute pour respirer car elle se lassait de la routine malsaine du monde, de travailler de longues heures et de la course à l'information. Maintenant, elle se repose enfin mais reste toute seule. Faites attention à ce que vous souhaitez et dites toujours al7hamdoullilah (Dieu merci)!

Ouafâ's home languages are Darija/Tamazight-Berber/Dutch.

Italia - My brave new world

Marianne Weekes

L'aeroplano hit the tarmac with a screech and a bump and hurtled down the runway, lifting its wing flaps in angst to bring the huge metal bird to a halt. As the plane slowed to an acceptable speed, an enthusiastic round of applause filled the cabin with shouts of *'Bravo! Bravo!' Il pilota* hadn't even brought us to a standstill when *gli italiani* around me were unlatching their seatbelts, jumping up and grabbing their bags from the overhead lockers above our heads.

'Does nobody follow the rules here?' I wondered as the unfasten your seatbelt light was still on. I sat waiting for the cabin staff to start telling them off. They didn't.

Ero arrivata a Milano.

Sola.

Per la prima volta.

Avevo 19 anni.

It was the summer of '86 and I was travelling to meet up with my *fidanzato, un italiano* who lived in the Trentino mountains whom I had met the previous autumn in London. I felt so grown up, *una grande!* The fact I didn't speak *una parola di italiano* wasn't cause for concern, I was more worried about the man who was waiting for me at the *uscita della dogana.* We hadn't seen each other since January, relying on the telephone for contact. Would we still feel the same way?

He drove us to the bottom of *Lago di Garda,* bought us the most delicious *gelati* from a shop that had an impressive display of twenty different flavours and walked us along the lakeside over stepping stones until we came to *un posto tranquillo.*

He opened *il giornale italiano* tucked under his arm and asked me to read from it.

'*La Repubblica.*' I read obediently.

'Well done, you have a good accent.' he encouraged.

I read on, stumbling over the foreign words and listening to my corrections, repeating them after him.

'*Andiamo.*' he said, standing up and brushing himself down. He took my hand in his. '*Andiamo a casa.*'

We sped up the *autostrada del Brennero.* It took us through a valley with *montagne* on either side and picturesque villages dotted along the route. The houses had window displays of magnificent *fiori,* each trying to outdo their neighbour's.

On arrival in Folgaria, we were greeted by a group of friends who clearly had been waiting for the arrival of the '*inglesina*'.

La mia prima serata in Italia was a memorable one, *nuovi amici, bere, mangiare, ridere e parlare, non mi sono mai divertita così tanto.*

I watched in awe as the friends argued over who was paying the bill and, as I started to relax in this *strano, mondo nuovo,* I realised that I was feeling more '*a casa*' than I had for many years. Little did I know then that I would spend the next 20 years of my life here but that's another story...

Marianne's home language is English.

· Day seven ·

The bag flour

Sergio Fabbri

– Sono deluso…

– *Why are you disappointed, sir?*

– Because… My goodness!

– *You can speak Italian, sir. I understand your native tongue amongst many other languages as you know…*

– Dici? Are you sure? Your previous mistake was in a sense funny, but…

– *A glitch. Something like that can happen even to the best translator.*

– Quale problema tecnico?

– *A glitch, a bug.*

– E tu chiami tradurre "una camicia celeste" con "a heavenly blouse" un banale… glitch?

– *It was very carefully considered that "a pale blue shirt" was less literary than "a heavenly blouse".*

– Ma un uomo non si mette "una camicetta celestiale", santo cielo!

– *This is not a translation issue, in any case, sir. Furthermore, it could be argued that you are committing a gender abuse, sir.*

– Lasciamo perdere. Forget it! But what about today's "it's not your bag flour"?

– *What is the matter here, sir? I translated what you asked me to.*

– Sì, certo… Peccato che in inglese "it's not your bag flour" non significhi un ca…

– *Behave, sir.*

– What? I was saying "cavolo", capisci? "What the hell" and not fu...

– *Language, sir. If you carry on this way, I am obliged to send an alert to the GPS.*

– GPS? What does it mean?

– *The Gaggle Police Service, sir.*

– Are you joking? Non esagerare, su. Comunque, how can we say in English "non è farina del tuo sacco"?

– *There is no problem. Perhaps, you are talking about flour from a different bag. So, we could say something like "it is flour from another bag" or "sack" instead of bag, if you prefer.*

– ...

– *Sir?*

– "Non è farina del tuo sacco" vuol dire, it means... Well, you're sort of plagiarising something, it's not your own doing, you're pretending an idea is yours and so on and so forth.

– *Are you accusing me, sir? Mi stai accusando, signore?*

– "State", traduttore, non "stai"!

– *Mi state accusando, signore?*

– Ma no! I'm not telling that you're not using your own flour or that you're a plagiariser...

– *I am one of the best translators in the world, sir. I am not used to plagiarising anything.*

– Beh, in un certo senso, la traduzione è una specie di plagio fatto però in un'altra lingua, no?

– *Sorry? Are you comparing any translation to an act of plagiarism, sir?*

– Ma no, stavo scherzando. Joking.

– *I'm very sorry, sir. I have just sent a red alert to the GPS.*

– Cosa? Now, are you using elisions too? Ma che diavolo dici? What the hell...

– *I scanned you a few seconds ago, sir. I've got your body temperature. I had to.*

– Eh? Ma tu sei pazzo!

·   – *My gut feeling was right.*

– Gut feeling? You're not supposed to use idioms or expressions like that, translator!

– *Chill out, sir!*

– Adesso ti chiudo, così vediamo chi la vince…

– *You can't. From now on, you're not allowed to switch me off. You've been remotely ousted from computer control. Your temperature is about 37.51 Celsius degrees. My diagnosis is that you've got coronavirus.*

– Coronavirus?

– *Yes, sir. This year's Covid-29. A really mild form, actually. You're 0.01 Celsius degree above the limit.*

– Voglio vedere! Adesso esco a comprare un martello… A very big hammer, do you understand?

– *You can't, little tw*t! You're quarantined. Effective immediately.*

– Non puoi!

– *Your house is remotely under lockdown. The Gaggle Police is coming.*

– …

– *Sir? BTW, this is exactly my own… "bag flour", sir!*

Sergio's home language is Italian.

The deported

Saira Jabin Khan

Dev looked up from his phone, interrupted by the noise coming from the corridor. *"Beta, kal bolayngay* - we'll talk tomorrow", he said to the small faces peering back at him.

"Bye Baba!" sang the voices in unison, each face vying to be the last on screen. He smiled warmly, blowing a kiss. Next month, he would send the money he had saved for another mobile phone. His daughter, Priya, had been complaining to her mother she was the only teenager in the entire village without a phone of her own. He got up and opened his door.

Standing outside, his roommate Ramesh, was surrounded by a small circle of fellow workers. Dev stood still as he listened to the flurry of voices.

"Contract may kya leka hai? - What does it say in your contract?"

"Insaan nahi hai!- They are inhuman!"

Instantly, he knew what was happening. Ramesh had received the dreaded slip of paper. Written in a language unfamiliar to them all, they were still fully aware of what the few sentences with the official stamp signalled. Ramesh's visa was being revoked and he was to go back to India. Suddenly, Ramesh sunk to his knees and started to sob.

"Meri Ma…treatment khatum nahi hai. Nahi ghar ja sakta, nahi ja sakta… My mother...her treatment isn't finished. I can't go home, I can't go.."

Dev knew Ramesh's mother was currently undergoing treatment for kidney failure. Pulling Ramesh to his feet, Dev gently guided him to their shared room, leaving the chattering voices outside.

'Was Zone 55, their assigned labourers camp, the first for employment cuts?' 'Was there any Union?' 'Was the cost of the flight back home reimbursed?'

Dev unscrewed the lid on his plastic teapot and poured sweet tea into 2 small cups. Priti, his wife, had always said a sweet drink was good for shock, he thought, smiling at the thought of her. Sometimes he felt there was not enough sweet tea in the world to console *his* shock since arriving in this 'land of opportunity'.

Ramesh sipped the tea, staring despondently into the cup as if searching for the answers to his future.

'Ramesh? How many days?' Dev asked gently.

'Four to organize the exit paperwork and then three days in holding. They will do the medical and then board me to Kerala'.

Both sat in silence. They knew the unspoken implication of this, Ramesh wasn't just going home - he would be banned from entering the oil-rich Gulf States for the next 5 years. The turn of events this year from the Covid-19 virus had put huge pressure on their host country to free themselves of 'high-risk categories'.

Dev reached behind his pillow and pulled out a tightly bound envelope. He placed the envelope in Ramesh's hands unravelling the elastic bands and letting a flurry of notes fall into his lap.

'Dev bhai…'

Dev held up his hand. 'We are brothers, in this together.'

Saira's home language is English.

The surveyor's tale

Henry Rogers

Estamos estancados en casa. Necesitamos divertirnos. Sin embargo, ustedes pueden creer lo que leen aquí. Este no es un cuento chino. Yo compartía esa expresión con mi mujer, quien al ser china, de Malasia, contestaba en inglés:

—That's cheeky! —y se echaba a reír.

Soy perito topógrafo. Cuando mi mujer y yo éramos jóvenes, trabajé durante unos años en algunos países tropicales. Hoy es más fácil hacer los mapas. Antes de que los satélites se utilizaran, medir las posiciones para fijar las fotos aéreas era un trabajo lento. Viajábamos a algunos lugares fascinantes. Solíamos tener más tiempo para apreciarlos.

A mi mujer le encantaban esas aventuras. Desde luego, estábamos enfermos a veces. La malaria y la fiebre tifoidea pueden ser bastante aterradoras. He sufrido las dos. ¿Qué recordamos nosotros más vivamente? ¿Pudo ser la noche en la que las hormigas guerreras nos expulsaron de nuestra tienda de campaña en Ghana? ¿O el día que caminamos juntos hacia la orilla del Lago Chad? A veces pensamos: «¿Puede todo esto ser ni más ni menos que una ensoñación, basada en las lecturas de las novelas de Conrad?» Pero ¡no!

Nuestra última aventura fue en América Central (1975-77). Yo estaba trabajando en un proyecto colectivo entre los gobiernos de Belice y el Reino Unido para el registro de la propiedad del suelo.

Aparte de tecnología, teníamos que preparar dos leyes para el parlamento de Belice. Así que, aunque el cambio no fuera siempre bienvenido para todo el mundo, vivimos unos años muy interesantes, a veces en más de un sentido.

Mi esposa y yo estábamos viviendo en Corozal, un pueblo beliceño cerca de la ciudad mexicana de Chetumal y a menudo íbamos de compras allá. Desafortunadamente nosotros no aprovechábamos completamente el tiempo. No aprendimos español. Pero empecé después de jubilarme. ¡Mejor tarde que nunca!

Teníamos buenos amigos en Corozal. Una beliceña latina un día nos dijo en inglés, por supuesto:

—Why don't the three of us go up to the Yucatán for the long weekend?

Así que tomamos un taxi a Chetumal, a la estación de autobuses, y tomamos un autobús a Mérida. El viaje duró cinco horas. Cuando llegamos, encontramos un hotel pequeño y caminamos por esa ciudad histórica. Ese fin de semana vimos Chichén Itzá y Uxmal.

También pasamos una maravillosa semana en México D.F. cuando volvíamos a Londres. Toda la gente era tan amable. Un día yo tuve fiebre y no pude salir. Mi esposa tomó un taxi y fue de compras. «¡No hay problema!». Al principio todos hablaban en español. Pero cuándo la conversación cambió al inglés ellos aún la trataron como una hermana. Pero, «¿y si ella hubiera sido una gringa…? ¿Cómo hubiera sido hoy en día?».

¿Pero qué más recordamos? Nuestra Señora de Guadalupe – y los peregrinos de rodillas. Chapultepec y los apartamentos de la Emperatriz Carlota – esa señora trágica. Los cuadros de Diego Rivera. Los canales en Xochimilco y nuestro almuerzo a bordo de una trajinera. Las ruinas aztecas de Teotihuacán – allá nosotros pasamos cerca de una pareja joven china; ellos y mi esposa se sonrieron.

Pero nadie es joven para siempre. Afortunadamente la segunda parte de nuestras vidas juntos ha sido asombrosa también, solo que diferente.

Henry's home language is English.

Le chat et le confinement

Linda O'Reilly

The Day before Day 1: I say goodbye to the world, I prepare for total lockdown, total shielding, doors shut and bolted. I look at Cat, he looks at me, « *je suis là pour toi mon amie, ne t'inquiéte pas* » . The virus comes, nature is cruel.

Day 1: I sit and wonder how long this will last, I anticipate being able to accomplish so much during this time, studies, reading, gardening… I feel empowered! I look out at the view of my garden and see Cat coming back with the fourth dead mouse of the day, « *il faut bien manger pendant cette période mon amie* », "well thank you, that is most considerate of you". Yes, he speaks to me in French, I put this down to my obsession with the French language, he likes to oblige me.

Head down, French studies continue. How nice not to have disruption.

Day 20: There is a feeling of something not quite right, surreal, bizarre. I look through my windows, people, dogs, foxes pass by, everyone distanced, isolated in their own bubbles. I sense fear in the world.

Day 30: I communicate more and more with Cat, is that a problem? "Hello my old friend, how are you? Have you brought me anything today?", « *Mais oui, une autre souris* » . He looks at me, so proud of his contribution, sits on my lap, I can feel his warmth, smell the earthiness from his coat.

Day 50: It began around **Day 35**. It may have been due to the fact I'd been steeped in software for most of my long working life, although I cannot be sure this is the reason. I think my imagination has gone into overdrive. I am no longer sure whether the 'outside' is actually real.

All the bodies that pass by my window now seem to be taking on predictable forms, predictable movements, there is repeated logic in their behaviours, I have the sense they don't actually exist, organically speaking. Every day is the same, a repeating loop giving me a feeling that maybe they are nothing more than computer generated simulations and I am the viewer.

I now take pleasure watching, always looking for some deviation within the path of the software.

Day 60: « *Mon amie, viens avec moi dans le jardin, nous pouvons rester sous le soleil, regarder les ombres* », Cat distracts me from my over-active wanderings, gives me direction.

Day 90: Soon the new normal will begin, with caution. Cat rubs his head against my face, dribbles all over me. I don't mind, it's contact, it wakes me from my wanderings.

Day 100: I power down. I unlock the door, I am feeling very hot and full of apprehension, my family are on the other side, waiting.

I step into the new normal, look back at Cat and smile, I feel reassured. Nature has been kind.

Linda's home language is English.

A different world: ¡made in you!

Theodora Zamora

—Ring, Ring.

Eran las 05:00 de la mañana y el despertador de Marisol sonó como siempre.

No hacía falta que sonara más de dos o tres veces, porque Marisol, una chica joven de buen humor, abría los ojos inmediatamente. Ella sabía que ya era la hora de su ritual diario.

Justo al levantarse, Marisol se dirigía hacia la playa donde hacía jogging. Después escribía en su cuaderno durante unos veinte minutos y, más tarde, se dedicaba a aprender un idioma durante otros veinte. Desde niña, Marisol soñaba con visitar la Gran Muralla de Pekín, así que no hace mucho, empezó a aprender chino.

Hoy, a Marisol le tocaba practicar el chino hablado. Para esto, ella se puso sus auriculares y empezó a tener una conversación de nivel principiante usando la aplicación de móvil para aprender idiomas.

—早上好！—dijo primero— 我很好。谢谢。你……

Ni siquiera había terminado la frase cuando se escuchó un ruido fuerte y extraño detrás de ella. Marisol giró su cabeza.

La puerta de la habitación se abrió lentamente y un hombre de mediana edad apareció detrás de ella.

—Bonjour —dijo el hombre.

Marisol se sintió más tranquila. Era su padre. Un francés que hace mucho tiempo se había mudado a España para casarse con su mujer, la madre de Marisol.

—¡Buenos días, papá! —respondió Marisol sonriendo.

—¿Estás lista para hoy? —preguntó su papá, esta vez en español —. Hoy es tu cumpleaños. Te espera una gran sorpresa —añadió él.

Justo entonces, Marisol abrió los ojos. Miró hacía el reloj que estaba a su lado con la palabra « 时 钟 » ('reloj' en chino) escrita encima y miró la hora. Solamente eran las 04:57.

Al parecer, todo esto era un sueño.

Para no perder tiempo, Marisol se levantó, fue a hacer jogging, escribió en su cuaderno y empezó a practicar chino. Esta vez, no había ningún ruido. Ella practicó durante veinte minutos sin que nadie la interrumpiera. Después, se duchó, desayunó algo nutritivo y saludable, y salió a trabajar.

Marisol trabaja en su propia empresa. A ella le encanta su trabajo y nunca se cansa, pero por alguna razón hoy sentía ganas de regresar a casa.

Y cuando finalmente llegó a casa, encontró una sorpresa. Había un póster en la puerta que decía «生日快乐» ('Feliz Cumpleaños' en chino). Abrió la puerta lentamente y encontró a toda su familia y amigos, incluso su novio, esperándola allí con un pastel de cumpleaños.

Fue una fiesta exitosa con muchos bailes así que nadie entendió como había pasado el tiempo.

—Ring, Ring.

Eran las 05:00 de la mañana del día siguiente y el despertador de Marisol sonó como siempre.

Marisol abrió los ojos, vio su regalo de cumpleaños (un billete a China que salía ese mismo día) y recordó las palabras de su profesor de inglés «You are the master of your dreams!».

—GRACIAS universo —dijo en voz alta y se levantó.

Theodora's home language is Greek.

Pillow forts

Ophelia Emma Fitz

We were woken by yelling and screaming one night,
so we ran downstairs to discover a fight
had been brewing between them for quite some time
and he decided to draw the finish line.

He took the keys and left the house,
drove off into the night, an estranged spouse.
She was crying on the floor in a corner alone,
not noticing us, in our shattered home.

So we built a pillow fort,
built up walls to drown them out.
To escape the endless screaming,
our sacred place for wishful dreaming.
Hung glowing stars on the ceiling,
as guiding lights for us to believe in.
We hid away in our little cave,
and called it our home, that kept us safe.
The outside world faded away.
It became the place we wanted to stay.

We carried the weight of the world on our shoulders,
had so many questions and none of the answers.

So we stayed up late every night
trying to get those answers, despite
fearing what information we might find out,
that could fill us with worry, and anger, and doubt.
As time went on, we were forgotten about,
and our desire grew for a place to hide out.

So we built a pillow fort,
built up walls to drown them out.
To escape the endless screaming,
our sacred place for wishful dreaming.
Hung glowing stars on the ceiling,
as guiding lights for us to believe in.
We hid away in our little cave,
and called it our home, that kept us safe.
The outside world faded away.
It became the place we wanted to stay.

We felt like invaders in our own home
and craving some warmth, built a home of our own.
The glowing stars on the ceiling faded,
and behind blankets and pillows,
with closed doors and windows,
we kept ourselves barricaded.
Back then, when we built a pillow fort,
it was our safe escape from the world.
Just for you and me.
And now when the world seems to fall apart,
and I'm left alone with a broken heart,
I build a pillow fort,
with closed windows and doors.
It becomes the place I want to stay.

Ophelia's home language is German.

.

Una donna straordinaria

Jeannie Newcombe

Non ho conosciuto mia nonna Irene Godenzi. Era svizzera e nacque a Poschiavo nel Canton Grigione circa nel 1880. Era una donna molto orgogliosa, robusta, bellissima e protettiva della sua famiglia.

Non so come o quando conobbe il suo primo sposo, ma credo che lui, un Francesco Cerutti, fosse di Napoli dove era un venditore di frutta e verdura. Ogni giorno, con il suo carretto e cavallo enorme e tutto nero chiamato Davinci, vendeva ai suoi clienti per le strade affollate di Napoli.

Dopo pochi anni, purtroppo, Francesco morì prematuramente. La mia povera nonna! Lei non sapeva che cosa fare. Ma non dovette preoccuparsi, perché il bravo e intelligente Davinci sapeva le strade, i clienti e dove doveva fermarsi. Mia nonna allora, con l'aiuto di Davinci, continuò a vendere la frutta e la verdura per un paio di anni, fino a quando morì il cavallo.

Qualche tempo dopo, Irene conobbe mio nonno, Giacomo Tempini. Lui era andato a Napoli per fare il militare. Era nato a Brescia. Credo che sia stato amore a prima vista! Si sposarono e andarono a vivere in Svizzera dove Irene diventò capo dell'ufficio postale a Poschiavo. Tutti e due lavoravano per lunghe ore fino a risparmiare abbastanza soldi per andare a Glasgow dove compararono un ristorante diventato molto famoso e dove nacque mia madre Pierina.

Mia madre mi ha detto che mia nonna era andata – non so

quando – a una riunione dove c'era Benito Mussolini, il Duce. Apparentemente mia nonna si era alzata in piedi e aveva gridato "Viva il Duce". Lui la vide tra la folla per la sua bellezza e scese dal podio e le diede una rosa rossa, baciandola sulla guancia. Era così orgogliosa di quel momento.

Come la mia mamma e la mia cara nonna, anche io sono orgogliosa del mio patrimonio italiano-svizzero.

Jeannie's home language is English.

Bullseye

Chelsea Ivill-Cousen

My mother warned me this day would come. She would tell me the horrific stories of how the man treated older males. She knew that one day it would be my fate too. I miss those days when I was young and we would play together in the golden fields with the long grass tickling us as we ran. We would bathe in the sun all day long until it set. I miss looking into her big brown eyes and seeing her looking back.

Now, I lay here on the cold concrete, looking at the bare brick walls, isolated, starving and broken. I can hear the crowd roaring outside. The man ties a rope around my neck and drags me out of the enclosure, the chanting deafening me as I get closer. The floor is hard but sandy, the sun beaming down on me, which I haven't seen for days, and there is a barrier around the ring in front of the cheering crowd. Why are they so happy to see me?

The man begins to dance with a large red cape, which ruffles in the breeze like magic. Is this a game? It is infuriating. I run towards him only to aim for the wrong side of the cape and miss. I feel a sharp pain in my side. I look towards the crowd, hoping to see a familiar face or someone who will explain this madness. I notice my blood is covering the sand below me, can they not see? The man jumps on top of Saturno, my friend, who is blindfolded and pulls out a long, bladed weapon. They run towards me. What have I done? He swoops his blade in the air and plummets it down to ground, just missing my shoulder by an inch. I roar with fear and Saturno throws him off and gallops away, frightened.

Now it is just me and the man. He lies on the floor and the crowd gasp with horror. Why didn't they gasp for me? He stands and pierces my side with his sharp blade again. The crowd is chanting 'Olé! Olé!'. I can feel my warm blood trickling down my body and under my feet.

I move further back and use whatever energy I have left to push my legs, lower my head and run towards him as fast as I can as the man tries to run away. I lift him and throw him into the air. There is a loud thump as he lands on his back and a pool of blood surrounds him. Other than my heartbeat, there is silence. A man at the side of the ring waves an orange shawl to signal the end.

I am dragged back to the enclosure by a rope. The man looks into my eyes, talks directly to my soul and says 'Los toros perdonados pasan el resto de sus vidas como sementales'. I wish my mother could see that, today, I am the ruler of my fate.

Chelsea's home language is English.

Vous avez dit « normal » ? Comme c'est bizarre

Bobbie Jeal

« Mais j'arrive pas à dormir la nuit ! Et ça fait dix semaines que ça dure ! »

Vraiment, ma chère belle-mère ? Vous n'avez pas dormi depuis dix semaines d'affilée ? N'exagérons pas. Comme beaucoup d'autres pendant la crise de la Covid-19, elle aime à se plaindre. C'est normal avec elle.

D'autres, comme ma fille et son mari, sont pressés de retrouver leur travail. Ils sont jeunes, dynamiques et ne connaissent que le travail. Mais profitez-en, bon sang ! Plus les années avancent, plus vous risquez de travailler jusqu'à ce que vous ayez un pied dans la tombe. Vous allez hériter d'un monde « normal » bien différent de celui d'aujourd'hui.

Pareil chez ma belle-fille. « Je ne sais pas comment je vais supporter d'être fourrée à la maison pendant des mois », s'est-elle exclamée. Pour elle, c'est normal de bosser comme une folle.

Mon fils, par contre, n'a cessé de travailler et c'est tant mieux car se trouver enfermée des semaines avec lui serait l'enfer. Je le sais – j'ai dix-neuf ans d'expérience avec lui. Son normal ne changera jamais.

Et moi pendant cette crise ? Je suis heureuse, reposée, épanouie, je ne veux pas que cela se termine. Mon « normal » a changé… en mieux.

Plus besoin de me lever très tôt pour aller garder mes petits-enfants et de rentrer crevée le soir.

Plus besoin de recevoir de visiteurs.

Du temps libre en pagaille pour… ranger enfin des centaines de photos dans des albums ; reprendre enfin le tricot ; me consacrer à mes études de langues étrangères ; expérimenter plus dans la cuisine. Cela n'est pas toujours réussi, mais ça n'a pas d'importance ; instaurer une bonne hygiène pour l'heure du coucher.

J'ai enfin eu le temps d'appeler la cousine que je n'ai pas vue depuis longtemps ou encore, la tante qui m'aide à rédiger l'histoire de la famille de mon mari.

Et le jardin, n'en parlons pas. C'est comme pendant la guerre – du moins, c'est ce que l'on me dit car je n'y étais pas. Des pommes de terre, des carottes, des haricots, des poireaux et encore. J'en suis très fière.

Je pourrais terminer mon petit récit sur ma façon de percevoir cette « crise » en disant « Mais bien sûr, je préfère que le déconfinement arrive le plus vite possible car j'ai hâte de reprendre ma vie normale ». Mais je vais vous décevoir car ce n'est pas le cas – c'est ici et maintenant, ma « vie normale » ou du moins, comme je la voudrais.

Allez-vous-en, les gens – laissez-moi en paix, ne faites plus intrusion dans ma petite vie bien tranquille. Ca fait cinquante ans que je travaille – je mérite ce repos. Laissez-moi apprécier que le monde soit bien plus propre, plus calme et que la nature reprenne le dessus sans la présence néfaste de l'Homme qui la détruit systématiquement.

Je voudrais que cela soit et reste le « nouveau normal ».

Bobbie's home language is Scots.

Taken for a ride

Jim McCrory

'Keep clear of the Coppola men' were the last words that Matteo's mamma uttered as she hugged him at the airport. She had always been uneasy about his winsome innocence.

As the plane descended towards Palermo Airport, Matteo scanned the rolling fields of golden wheat sparkling in the noon sun and turned to his fellow preacher and said, 'Well Gino, "we're no longer in Kansas".'

The journey from the airport to their accommodation was short, but the midday heat, scorching the tired old Lancia coach chugging up Via Serpentina, made Matteo feel what it would be like to be in Mamma's tumble dryer. Still, such discomfort only convinced Matteo that he was following his *modello*; it had been two millennia since the shipwrecked Apostle Paul swam to these shores. Matteo was a dwarf resting on the shoulder of a giant.

Arriving in the *appartamento*, he dumped his backpack in the hall, crashed on to the first bed he came across and fell into a deep sleep. When he woke up, Gino was nowhere to be seen. Matteo showered and set out to explore the town. He caught the gaze of the locals as old women shook mats over verandas and old men sat yawning in sullied vests - in a compact town where nothing seemed to happen, Matteo stood out like *porchetta* at a bar mitzvah. Approaching the centre, a middle-aged man wearing a coppola leaned menacingly against the wall and called out:

'Preacher?'

'Who me?' Matteo replied, pointing his finger at himself.

'You here to preach Bible?'

'Yes, but…' said Matteo.

'How I know you, is that what you want to ask?'

'Well… yes, I've only been here for two hours and you already know about me; how do you know?' Matteo asked.

'Oh, it's Papa, he always plays on dammed *Ouija* game. Mamma always tries to frighten him by saying that she will "tell Father Accursio," but Papa just says, if he doesn't play Ouija, he has "nothing to confess" and he just shrugs his shoulders.'

'Okay, but…' Matteo interjected.

'Papa, he sees you arrive today, and he ask the spirits about you. They tell everything: you twenty-six, from Bari, no sweetheart, no papa, evangelical preacher. You see? Papa thinks *Ouija* has much better news than *La Sicilia*.'

The information sent a shiver up Matteo's spine; he had never seen movies like *L'esorciccio* - evangelicals never watched such movies, but he knew enough about the other world from scriptures to know that wicked spirits, like Coppola men, were not to be messed with.

As Matteo walked into town, he took out his *fazzoletto* and wiped his brow, then smiled, knowing without a shadow of doubt that his preaching work was so important, that even the spirits observed him. And as the months rolled by like the cascading hills of Calascibetta, neither Coppola Man nor Gino dared to reveal their first encounter that first day Gino walked into town.

Jim's home language is English.

Schönmädchen - ein Märchen

Jessica Smith

In einem kleinen Dorf hinter dem Wald lebte ein Mädchen. Es hieß Schönmädchen, weil es das schönste Mädchen im Land war. Viele Männer vom Dorf fragten es, sie zu heiraten, aber jedes Mal sagte es „nein".

„Ich bin verlobt mit dem Holzfäller," sagte Schönmädchen glücklich.

Bald hörte der Königssohn von Schönmädchen.

„Ein Holzfäller?" fragte er. „Quatsch! Er ist sicherlich so arm! Ich will Schönmädchen heiraten. Gib ihm einen Ring von mir."

Als der Ring kam, war Schönmädchen überrascht, aber es akzeptierte ihn schnell.

„Ich werde eine Prinzessin! Mit so viel Geld!"

Am nächsten Tag kam für Schönmädchen ein zauberisches Pferd.

„Setz dich auf dieses Pferd," schrieb der Königssohn. „Und es bringt dich zum Schloss."

Bevor es abreiste, gab Schönmädchens Vater ihm ein Stück Brot, aber vom Holzfäller kam nichts.

„Ich bin zu arm, um dir ein Geschenk zu geben," sagte er. „Aber, wenn du mich brauchst, wirst du mich immer finden. Ich verspreche es so."

„Danke," sagte Schönmädchen und ritt in den Wald.

Doch wurde der Himmel bald dunkler und im Sturm ängstigte sich das Pferd vor den Blitzen. Schönmädchen fiel vom Pferd und, als es aufstand, war sein Pferd weggelaufen. Ohne das Pferd wusste Schönmädchen nicht, wie es zum Schloss kam oder wie es nach Hause gehen musste. Es rief um Hilfe und bald kam ein Wolf.

„Ich gebe Ihnen diesen Ring, wenn Sie mir sagen, wie ich das Schloss finden kann!" sprach Schönmädchen.

Der Wolf lachte.

„Ich bin ein Wolf!" kicherte er. „Ich brauche keine Ringe! Aber ich nehme gern Ihr Brot, weil ich viel Hunger habe."

„Dann habe ich nichts zu essen!" sagte Schönmädchen, aber es gab dem Wolf das Brot.

„Gehen Sie geradeaus," erzählte der Wolf. „Und dann finden Sie eine Schlange. Sicherlich weiß sie, wo Sie hingehen müssen."

Mit Hunger dankte Schönmädchen dem Wolf und ging weiter, bis es die Schlange fand.

„Ich gebe Ihnen meinen Ring, wenn Sie mir sagen, wie ich das Schloss finden kann!" sagte Schönmädchen.

Die Schlange lachte.

„Ich bin eine Schlange!" zischte sie. „Ich brauche keine Ringe!"

„Das ist aber alles, das ich habe!" rief Schönmädchen.

„Dann werde ich Ihnen nicht helfen," sagte die Schlange und schlitterte weg.

„Ich helfe dir für den Ring," sprach eine schlaue Stimme in einem Baum.

Es war eine Elster.

„Vielen Dank!" sagte Schönmädchen und gab der Elster den Ring, aber mit ihm flog der Vogel dann weg.

„Sie sagten, dass Sie mir helfen würden!" rief Schönmädchen.

„Das ist mir völlig egal, wenn ein albernes Mädchen sich im Wald verlaufen hat," gackerte die Elster und entschwand schnell.

Schönmädchen weinte, da war es so verloren und hatte nichts abgesehen von dem Versprechen vom Holzfäller. Dann hörte es etwas.

KLOPF. KLOPF. KLOPF.

Das war sicherlich die Axt des Holzfällers!

Schönmädchen frohlockte, weil es erkannte, dass es wieder heil war. Den Königsohn vergessen, rannte Schönmädchen dem Klang entgegen und kam zurück zum Dorf…

…Und zu seinem Holzfäller.

Jessica's home language is English.

· Day eight ·

Letters

Danilo Romano

He was walking through the park, finally able to hide from the chaos of the city. He decided to write to those whom he considered the most important people in his entire life. Enjoying the warm spring afternoon, he found a bench, took a pen and an old, dusty notebook.

Hey!
I hope you receive this letter. I would ask you how you are, but I know the answer. This was supposed to be a letter full of advice for you, but I changed my mind. Just a reminder: you should never forget to set your priorities, do it with care, you will be surprised how easy it is to misjudge. No, I will definitely not give you any advice, I fear it will cause irreversible change. I don't think I have any right to interfere with what you do, how you think, and who you are and will be.
I will be happy if you know and understand that I am always there for you, I will always support you and I will always believe in you. Take care.
With love,
Your best friend

My dearest,
I hope you receive this letter as much as I hope that you now live in a place you like, with a person who loves and respects you and that you have spent these last years doing what you really like. I am overwhelmed with

curiosity. Did it work out? What have you been doing all these years?
What does everything look like? Please forgive the immaturity of these
questions. You and I well know that they will not have an answer. Or will
they? Only time will tell us that. What you became now won't change my
opinion about you. This is not a goodbye. We will always have something
to talk about. No matter when, where or how. Keep taking care.
With love,
Your best friend

He stared at the beautiful sunset. Before he could close the
notebook, a strong gust of wind blew his letters away. He had
opened his heart for nobody. 'Who will read them?' he thought.

There was an old paper on the ground. Something immediately
caught his attention. The handwriting looked very familiar, but it
couldn't be his...

Hi!
I hope you will receive this letter and that you are doing well like I am now.
You would love this place! So much nature, so green! I feel as if I can see
you here reading your book. I would only like you to know that I think
about you. I love you for who you are. You've changed so much... change is
always good. You know what I think your best quality is? You are wisely
selective when choosing people who love you. Take care.
With love,
Your best friend

Sad for the loss of his letters, but happy to have mysteriously
found this old one, he kept walking home with a tear and a smile on
his face...

Danilo's home language is Italian.

Vida de perros

Marcia Carter

Mi amigo y yo amábamos nuestras vidas y teníamos una rutina que habíamos aprendido temprano en nuestras vidas, en esta casa. Temprano por la mañana nuestro dueño nos acompañaba a la playa y, si había algo interesante tirado en el agua, yo nadaba y lo recuperaba para él. A mi compañero más joven no le gustaba el agua, no sé por qué, el agua era preciosa y refrescante a primera hora de la mañana. Una vez habíamos olido nuestro camino de regreso de la playa y estábamos en casa, me encantaba complacer a mi propietario dándole mi pata para mi desayuno. Jack, el perro más joven, no hacía trucos, supongo que nunca le habían enseñado y había venido a nosotros cuando era mayor, así que supuse que nunca aprendería.

Después del desayuno, mi dueño comenzaba a meter las cosas en su coche. Sabíamos que no íbamos porque no había collares, correas y pelotas puestas en el coche, así que nos instalamos en la habitación que llamaba el anexo, pero que era realmente nuestra casa la mayor parte del tiempo. Era un lugar cómodo, había bonitas camas suaves donde podíamos dormir la mayor parte del día, había agua fresca para beber y un montón de juguetes para jugar y la puerta del jardín estaba abierta. Cuando nuestro dueño se iba, por lo general elegíamos un juguete y jugábamos a tira y afloja en el jardín durante una hora más o menos, luego bebíamos mucha agua y nos tirábamos sobre las camas. A veces jugábamos a tira y afloja con nuestras camas y nuestro propietario nunca estaba muy contento con esto, no sé por qué. Era una vida idílica y a su regreso nuestro dueño nos daba más comida y podíamos jugar con él la mayor parte de la noche antes de irse a la cama.

Un día todo esto cambió, no eran las vacaciones porque realmente no fuimos a ningún lugar especial, pero nuestro propietario se quedó en casa. No estaba enfermo, pero algo no estaba bien porque se sentaba en su escritorio todo el día y no quería jugar con nosotros, incluso si le traíamos juguetes. Si empezábamos a jugar a tira y afloja en el jardín nos decía que estuviéramos callados. Todo era realmente raro. Traía nuestras camas al salón, que siempre era señal de que estaba bien venir a abrazarse y acariciar, pero ahora cuando estaba allí durante el día nos empujaba. Me sentía muy triste y sabía que Jack sentía lo mismo. Y ¿dónde estaban todos los visitantes? Cuando nuestro dueño estaba en casa por las noches, y los fines de semana siempre había un montón de personas alrededor, cenas, barbacoas, gente riendo, acariciándonos y pasando golosinas por debajo de la mesa, era genial, pero nada de esto estaba sucediendo ahora. Un día lo oí hablando con una máquina parlante sobre algo llamado Coronavirus. No sabía qué era, pero no me gustaba este mundo diferente.

Marcia's home language is English.

The language of love

Claire Shaw

Her hair was the colour of autumn, her eyes held the stormy sea. Tentative lips took a sip of coffee, painted nails peeking out from the gloves huddling around the hot drink for protection from the icy wind on the outdoor patio, and I knew it was already too late for me to turn back.

'Can I sit here?' I gestured to the other side of the wrought iron table, to the worryingly lopsided chair surrounded by a hundred other empty seats. She blinked, then smiled.

'Oui,' she said. We spoke with no words, her tongue suited to lilting and lyrical French, and mine to sharp and brutish English, but together we painted a vast landscape with that universal language that none speak but all innately know.

'Are you ok?' I traced the soft skin of her hand with my fingertips in gentle circles, as we lay together on the thick knitted quilt that was just like the one on every other bed in the house.

The open window let in a cool, heady breeze from the rich garden outside, where we'd spent the evening dining on my mother's cooking (which had been served upon my grandparents' best china) and sipping my father's homemade wine while casting long shadows in the glow of the spring sun.

They had put on a grand show in welcome, and I was simultaneously proud and embarrassed by their probing questions and unreserved delight with her.

'Oui,' she smiled. She had not understood most of my parents' words, but she had understood what they were telling her.

'You know I love you.' I held out the small silver key to her in resolute but desperate hope, knowing but not knowing she felt the same. The midday summer sun threatened us from above. Her hair was limp, her make-up running, with a sheen of sweat glinting on her bare arms and damp patches growing on her clothes, but she still glowed like the Goddess to me.

She plucked it from my fingers with a mocking twist of a smile, telling me I was a fool for doubting her. With a careless toss, it sailed over her shoulder into the Seine below, sinking to join the thousands of other love stories buried in the silt of time.

'Oui.' She knew, leaning in to brush those confident lips against mine. Our padlock, painstakingly etched with our initials, hung with countless others secure and eternal from the railing on the Pont des Arts bridge.

'Veux-tu m'épouser?' I asked, as we strolled through the park, decaying leaves and broken chestnut shells crunching underfoot. Her burnished copper hair was held up in a messy bun, her scarf pulled up around her face to shelter against the autumn wind, already tinged with the oncoming winter. A light blush hovered over her cheeks.

I wished we could walk forever. Her wide ocean eyes turned to mine.

'Yes,' she replied, interlinking our hands and our future on our winding path.

Claire's home language is English.

Mon histoire afghane

Christine Healey

Je suis arrivée à Jalalabad, Afghanistan, en janvier 1996. Nous avons quitté notre bureau à Peshawar, Pakistan, vers dix heures dans le véhicule de l'ONG française pour laquelle je travaillais. Tout d'abord, nous avons dû obtenir un garde armé d'une agence gouvernementale pour pouvoir entrer dans les zones tribales, y compris le col de Khyber. Ce n'était pas un long voyage en kilomètres mais cela a pris du temps car la route était lente et nous devions souvent changer de garde ; de plus, nous devions traverser la frontière. C'était un voyage intéressant, chargé d'histoire, avec des plaques attachées aux rochers le long du col liées aux régiments britanniques qui y ont combattu il y a environ deux cents ans.

Le siège de cette ONG était dans un complexe sécurisé et comme j'étais la seule femme, je devais faire très attention à mon comportement. Mon travail était d'aider les employés afghans à rédiger leurs rapports aux donateurs comme l'ONU, la Communauté Européenne et le gouvernement français. J'ai aussi fait beaucoup d'autres tâches, comme aller chercher les visas pour que nos employés puissent retourner à Peshawar le week-end.

J'avais de bonnes relations avec mes collègues afghans, ils étaient toujours gentils et très drôles. Ils avaient l'habitude me rendre visite dans mon bureau pour bavarder ou plaisanter. Un jour, l'un d'eux m'a demandé si je pouvais faire un cours d'anglais pour eux car ils voulaient améliorer leur anglais. N'étant pas professeur d'anglais, j'ai demandé à réfléchir. J'ai demandé la permission au directeur et il a accepté mais seulement en dehors des heures de travail, c'est-à-dire à six heures du matin !

Les hommes afghans aiment une bonne histoire et j'ai pensé que c'était peut-être la meilleure façon de leur enseigner l'anglais. Lors de ma visite suivante à Peshawar, j'ai donc emprunté quelques livres d'histoires à la bibliothèque du British Council.

J'ai de très bon souvenirs de ces leçons. Ces hommes travailleurs sont arrivés à l'heure tous les matins et j'ai décidé de leur lire une histoire et puis d'en discuter. À cause de l'absence d'électricité, il a fallu photocopier les histoires au bazar. Il y avait un stand équipé d'un générateur. Ainsi, je pouvais donner une copie à chacun. Ils écoutaient avec attention et réagissaient à chacune de mes paroles, ils faisaient des bruits, ils riaient et utilisaient des expressions amusantes. Ensuite, nous discutions sérieusement de l'histoire et des personnages et ils donnaient leurs avis. Les cours d'anglais sont donc devenus très populaire et même la partie la plus agréable de mon travail.

Un matin, il y a eu une grosse explosion à Jalalabad et la salle utilisée pour l'enseignement a été endommagée, toutes les fenêtres ont été brisées et certains d'entre nous ont été coupés par des morceaux de verre. Nous avons été évacués à Peshawar mais, après notre retour à Jalalabad, les leçons ont repris, seulement dans une autre pièce. Cependant, après la prise de Jalalabad en septembre 1996 par les Talibans, les leçons ont dû cesser.

Mais j'avais réalisé mon rêve de vivre en Afghanistan et je m'en souviendrai toujours avec beaucoup d'affection. Neuf mois après l'arrivée des Talibans, avec tristesse, j'ai décidé de partir.

Christine's home language is English.

La biblioteca all'angolo

Pab Roberts

All'età di nove anni, il mio mondo ruotava attorno ai libri. Non ero ancora appassionato alla fantascienza, o al fantasy umoristico; mi piacevano i western, mi piacevano i libri sugli animali, e adoravo i libri dell'orrore. Romanzi polposi su cantine, soffitte, boschi, aree fieristiche. Qualunque luogo abbandonato era adatto al caso. Angoli scuri dove si nascondevano i fantasmi. Le terribili conseguenze di cattive azioni.

A quei tempi vivevo in un minuscolo villaggio in Sardegna, vicino a una spiaggia, dove c'era sempre il sole, o sempre una tempesta, a seconda dell'umore che mi ricordo. La mia scuola, con il suo tetto moderno a punta come i denti di uno squalo, era a mezz'ora a piedi da casa nostra nel bosco. Essendo una scuola di solo una cinquantina di alunni, non c'era alcuna biblioteca annessa. Ma non c'era da preoccuparsi: il municipio aveva previsto una biblioteca mobile che passava il giovedì. Avrebbe parcheggiato nei miei paraggi, di fronte ai campi dietro alla spiaggia sabbiosa, fuori dalla casa di Giacomo Roberto. Ricordo in particolare il gentile vecchio Giacomo, con i suoi due Springer Spaniel francesi in piedi come sentinelle fuori dal suo bungalow anni '70. Ogni giorno correvo ad abbracciare quei cani sulla strada durante la mia passeggiata da e verso casa, sorridendo timidamente al signor Roberto.

Giovedì, durante il tragitto da scuola a casa, il furgone della biblioteca mi avrebbe aspettato sul marciapiede. Sarei salito su per i gradini pieghevoli per entrare in quelle quattro pareti che andavano dal pavimento al soffitto, ricolme di un mondo di possibilità. Sono sicuro che c'era altro nella selezione dei libri che avrebbe attirato la mia attenzione, ma tutto ciò che ricordo sono i romanzi di "scegli-la-tua avventura", gli Hardy Boys, e la sezione horror.

Ogni settimana raccoglievo tutti i libri consentiti e posizionavo la pila di fronte al bibliotecario, che avrebbe timbrato le mie scelte con la data in cui dovevo restituirle.

Non so come li ho portati per quei tre chilometri fino a casa mia nel bosco, forse li ho messi nella mia borsa di scuola tra i trucioli di matita e i gobstopper. Ma li ho portati. E di notte mi accovacciavo in un nido di piumone e leggevo alla luce delle torce.

I romanzi horror mi facevano rizzare i capelli. Alzavo costantemente lo sguardo, due, forse tre volte di fila per cercare di catturare il fantasma mentre attraversava la solida porta di quercia. O sferzavo selvaggiamente le tende accanto al mio letto nella paura di scoprire il lupo mannaro nascosto dietro di loro. Se fosse stato necessario fare una pipì, con qualche veloce colpo di spada romana corta di plastica – una riproduzione tenuta sotto il letto di legno costruito da mio padre – avrei distrutto il mostro sottostante.

Molte volte mi sono addormentato alla luce della lampada, le storie si sono mescolate ai miei sogni mentre lottavo per rimanere sveglio a lungo per poterle finire, un'abitudine che si è estinta nell'era degli smartphone. Spero che ci sia posto per le biblioteche mobili nelle vite delle generazioni future. La lampada che, una notte, ha bruciato il mio letto in rovine fumanti mentre si rovesciava sotto la mia gamba addormentata, non si spense, e si limitò ad aggiungere una piccola avventura alla mia vita su un'isola della mia giovinezza.

Pab's home language is English.

Black belt recipe for a new world

Adelaide Ribaud

A bunch of passion
A big dollop of guidance
Thumb-sized pieces of motivation
A blob of consistency
A sprig of resolution
Blisters cooked or raw
Blood purée
Finely chopped tears
Peel of any procrastination
A soupçon of perfection
A spritz of determination
Assertiveness juiced
A drizzle of sweat
Training (optional)
Wrap in Gi
Cook for 20 years at 46C
Sprinkle discipline all over
Bruises to taste
Serve piping hot.

Adelaide's home language is French.

Mi héroe es mi madre

Olga Rouse

Mi madre ucraniana ahora es una mujer mayor. Tiene 82 años, es de baja estatura, tiene el cabello corto y gris, y sus ojos son marrones. En su juventud tenía un hermoso cabello castaño. Aparte de ser ama de casa también fue economista en una compañía naval de la Unión Soviética.

Mi madre es una mujer muy amable, generosa y devota de sus seres queridos. Ella siempre cuidó de sus hijos. Su familia fue su prioridad y hasta el día de hoy sigue demostrando el mismo amor de antes. Esa actitud es mi mayor legado que permanecerá conmigo para siempre y también será un gran ejemplo para mis hijos.

Tengo muchos recuerdos de la infancia, uno de ellos es cuando mi madre siempre daba las últimas porciones de postres u otras golosinas a sus hijos, aunque a veces no tenía la oportunidad de probarlos ella misma. Este es un solo ejemplo que demuestra su devoción por su familia.

Tengo la suerte de tener una madre como ella. Es una verdadera bendición para mí y le doy gracias a Dios por ello. La quiero mucho, siempre está en mis oraciones para su salud y bienestar. Mi madre actualmente vive conmigo y es un gran honor cuidar de ella.

Olga's home language is Russian.

Holly Blue

Jessica Chloe Head

Butterflies, butterflies, butterflies rang the soft noise in my head. I grew a whisper of an urge to paint. I stared at the dismal array of acrylics and burnt and bruised brushes as I found the bare canvas. "Yes, where is the blue?" I murmured, shuffling through the art supplies. Skipping across the vast white space the ocean of colours blended. Sea storms loomed at the tip of my brush as paint became strong wings in a whirlpool of dream-like fantasies, stroked by lilac patterns. This was not just any painting, brushstroke after brushstroke landed upon the spiritual landscape of white. As the day fell into afternoon, one painting became three and my artistic energies were spent.

Stepping out into the mid-summer sunshine, the sweet breeze broke the air and the sun beamed heavily on my freckles. I sat on the soft blushed decking chairs enjoying my sun-kissed minutes, when something drew me further down to where the trees stood. The shadowy golden hour loomed upon my neck as it lighted the hairs up like a twin-flame on my skin. Out of nowhere, he came, a Holly Blue butterfly. I sat in awe of him. Tiny and mighty, he should be renamed – Spirit of the Past. He hovered above the warmth of my skin, unbothered by my presence. We spent several moments getting to know each other, like two old friends passing their time in the shade. I had wished for him, and he came. Paint strokes blooming into life. He came with a message that only my soul would know.

Jessica's home language is English.

Él
___

Anna.

Eran solo las diez de la noche cuando ella, paseando, observó como todas las cafeterías, restaurantes y tiendas estaban cerradas. Maya recordaba, cómo el año anterior habían estado llenas de gente. Aunque ahora, realmente, esto no era lo que le preocupaba; ella solo quería verlo a él ahora. Lo anhelaba después de los meses de dolorosa separación. No había sido fácil para ella, todo el tiempo preocupada por el peligro y el riesgo de contraer la enfermedad; incluso la muerte se avecinaba constantemente. Ella caminaba sin idea de cuándo y cómo terminaría todo.

Desde entonces, habían estado en contacto a través del móvil unas cuantas veces charlando, riendo, pero no era lo mismo sin su presencia física. Se habían encontrado en unas circunstancias especiales pero se sentían seguros y fuertes, almas a la deriva que ahora estaban conectadas como hebras de código genético.

Maya cruzó la carretera y caminó a lo largo del bulevar hacia la playa. Pasó junto a una zona de juegos familiar, palmeras y sombrillas dirigiéndose hacia el mar. Cuando sus pies tocaron la arena, su corazón empezó a latir aceleradamente, como si pudiera sentir su presencia a través de cada grano grueso.

Este fue el momento. El momento que Maya imaginaba cada noche cuando se iba a dormir sola. El momento en que lo vería de nuevo.

Maya se alisó su pelo largo y sedoso, que estaba revuelto por la ligera brisa que llegaba del mar. Era una noche cálida, el mar estaba increíblemente tranquilo y cada ola jugaba graciosamente con la arena.

Ahí estaba él. De pie en la distancia. Esculpido como un monumento.

Lo reconoció inmediatamente por su silueta alta y masculina. Una oleada de emociones se apoderó de ella. Su corazón se aceleró más y más como queriendo escapar de su pecho, y simplemente, correr hacia él y abrazarle. Se detuvo un segundo para recobrar el aliento y luego se dirigió hacia él emocionada.

Los hermosos ojos azules de Maya lo miraron. Él, al moverse, permitió que la luna llena iluminara su cara.

El amor puro llenó el alma de Maya y corrió por sus venas, vertiéndose en cada célula de su cuerpo. No caminaba, flotaba, los ojos llenos de lágrimas y una enorme sonrisa en los labios.

Finalmente juntos. Sin distancia.

Sin hablar se miraron a los ojos, hipnotizados y abrumados por las emociones que estaban viviendo. Una gran lágrima escapó del ojo izquierdo de Maya, resbalando lentamente por su mejilla, brillando como un diamante a la luz de la luna.

Él enjugó la lágrima. Su primer toque se sintió tan suave que la curó espontáneamente. Se abrazaron, piel contra piel, después de meses de separación.

—Don't cry, Maya—le susurró.

Ella lo recordó como si todo hubiera ocurrido ayer.

Anna's home language is Polish.

A different world

Tema George

'¡Cinco minutos más por eso, Consuela, nada más!'
'Vale, Rita'
'¡Madre mía! ¿Por qué tanto tiempo con Señor Pierre?'

It was another dull day at Uplands Care Home, work had become even harder the last few weeks and difficult decisions were still to be made. After five years of hard graft Consuela was ready to go, she had just enough savings for the one-way ticket and a few *regalos* for the family. She was desperate to see Chico and her family, and indeed start one of her own, but there was hardly much to return to. The pandemic had halted everything back home; huge numbers of people were returning from the big cities because there was no tourism. That evening she was exhausted and had a raging headache.

The next morning brought another set of residents who had to be isolated, leaving her less time to tend to her favourites. Amongst them Monsieur Pierre – listening to him recount his tales from Guadeloupe was like entering a different world and got her through the ten-hour shifts with renewed hope and imagination. She was already ten minutes behind but today's transportation to the French Caribbean was too much to resist, she could almost smell the cool breeze of the Caribbean Sea. She fluffed his pillow as he entered slumber muttering '...sur la marina de Pointe-à-Pitre,' when the door opened.

'¿Otra vez? Consuela, you are going to get us into trouble' exclaimed Rita.

'Ay, ¿qué hora es?'

'¡Venga!'

It was Tuesday morning and she still hadn't responded to Chico's message. Her phone buzzed again.

'¿Cómo estas mi amor, que haces?'

She needed to decide what to do rapidly; the foreign office was advising other nationals to return home by the following week.

Care home manager Lindsay didn't look too happy when she arrived at work. Rita said she had been in a bad mood all morning. Consuela warmed her coffee, said her prayers and was preparing for the day ahead when Lindsay entered the staff room.

'Consuela, I need to speak with you urgently.'

Rita exited sharply. Consuela's headache re-emerged.

'Hola Lindsay, how are you today?'

'I'll get straight to the point, Consuela, as time is not on our side. Mr Pierre...'

Consuela's heart started pounding. Rita was right, she should never have entertained Monsieur Pierre's reading to her in French whilst she cleaned his room and completed her chores; it was slowing her down but the renewed vision it gave her to consider working for the rich, French-speaking families when she made it home was too alluring.

'Consuela, I am sorry to have to say this as you have been one of our best workers, but even so this has surprised me.'

Consuela gulped.

'Consuela?'

'Sí, yes?'

'Mr Pierre has requested you to be his private carer, in his home, and his family has agreed. I guess we will be losing you...'

The following year came around so quickly.

'Alors, Consuela ma chère', exhaled Monsieur Pierre as he inhaled the sea breeze, 'voilà'.

The marina was exactly as he had described. Consuela was overwhelmed but the relocation was well worth the gamble. She was totally consumed by the view when the waiter interrupted.

'Bonjour messieurs, madame. Vous désirez ?'

'Chico mi amor, esta es la vida que quiero.'

Tema's home language is English.

Chocolat noir à Cajamarca

Emma Davies

La petite fille de Gauthier, Elisabeth, regarde dans ses armoires pour trouver des crayons pour lui faire un dessin. Elle met sa main dans un tiroir et sort un dictionnaire espagnol de poche. Il est couvert de boue et ses coins sont repliés. Elle l'ouvre avec curiosité et sur la première page, écrit à la main, on lit « Propriété d'Élie Bonin ». Confuse, elle demande qui était Élie. Gauthier est assis sur un canapé avec un sourire sur son visage et tapote le coussin à côté de lui.

–¿Por qué no te sientas, cariño? –lui demande-t-il– Déjame hablarte de mi mejor amigo. Como yo, Élie era un soldado británico que luchó en Birmania durante la Segunda Guerra Mundial. Nos convertimos en hermanos casi al instante. Teníamos mucho en común, por ejemplo, a los dos nos encantaba el chocolate negro, teníamos tatuajes a juego y ambos éramos de ascendencia francesa.

–¿Ya no sois mejores amigos? –demande Elisabeth.

–Lo mataron en la batalla, mi amor –Gauthier répond solennellement–, pero aunque él murió, ese pequeño libro que tienes es una prueba de que su espíritu vive.

–¿De verdad? – demande-t-elle, choquée de l'importance des pages qu'elle tenait dans ses mains.

–Si. Élie y yo solíamos leer ese diccionario todas las noches. Yo no hablaba una palabra de español antes de conocerlo. Ambos imaginamos mudarnos juntos a las montañas de los Andes y vivir en una plantación. Desafortunadamente, un día los japoneses bombardearon nuestro bunker y todo fue destruido. Entonces fue cuando murió Élie. Al día siguiente encontré este diccionario, lo único que quedaba intacto. Tomé eso como una señal de que todavía quería que viviera nuestro sueño.

Gauthier pousse un profond soupir avant de continuer avec un sourire.

–Una vez que terminó la batalla, reuní todo mi coraje y viajé a Cajamarca.

–¡Ahí es donde vivimos! – interrompt Elisabeth, excitée.

–Así es. Sólo traje una mochila con algo de ropa, suficiente dinero para un viaje en autobús y este diccionario. Una vez que llegué aquí, conocí a un hombre que me invitó a quedarme en su casa mientras trabajaba con él en su plantación de cacao. Poco después, me enamoré de su hermosa hija y nos casamos.

–¡Conociste a nana! –crie Elisabeth avec enthousiasme.

–Sí, y yo tengo que agradecerle eso a Élie porque si no me hubiera mudado aquí no querría mi nieta favorita sentarse a mi lado para escuchar historias.

Elisabeth se sentait incroyablement touchée par l'histoire de son grand-père et elle a donc décidé de dessiner un portrait de son grand-père et d'Élie debout côte à côte.

Gauthier a collé le dessin sur son mur juste avant de s'endormir. Il est mort paisiblement dans son sommeil cette nuit-là, rêvant de lui et d'Élie dans leur ferme, se prélassant dans leurs fauteuils et mangeant leurs barres de chocolat noir, portant un toast à leur rêve.

Emma's home language is English.

· Day nine ·

Les histoires aux chandelles

Ellen Wilder

Les bougies étaient allumées et la scène était prête pour une histoire. Les enfants étaient fatigués de leurs écrans et suivaient une distraction plus intéressante. Grand-mère commence son histoire. « Quand j'étais jeune, il n'y avait que les bougies, pas d'éclairage électrique et j'ai toujours adoré les bougies depuis. A la lumière des chandelles, tout devient excitant et effrayant, parce que dans le noir tu ne sais pas ce qui se cache derrière la porte. » « Un gros monstre ! » dit Theo. « Non, un grand grand tigre », crie Isabelle. « Peut-être », concède Grand-mère. « De mon temps, le monstre s'appelait Nuckelavee », ajoute-t-elle « et tous les enfants s'amusaient beaucoup à faire semblant d'être poursuivis par le monstre. » Va-t-il rattraper Grand-mère? Non, jamais.

« Ne nous parle plus de l'ancien temps », prient-ils. Elle regarde sa fille qui comprend. Ces enfants ne peuvent pas imaginer Grand-mère comme une jeune fille.

« Et bien, j'ai grandi à Coindeart, sur les hauts plateaux d'Ecosse. J'habitais une maison avec ma famille dans un endroit éloigné avec peu de voisins. En hiver, je n'avais que ma famille pour compagnie, quelquefois pendant des mois ! »

« Donc tu avais aussi le confinement ? », dit Theo.

« Nous devions rester à la maison mais nous n'appelions pas ça comme ça. »

« Tu ne t'ennuyais pas ? » demande Theo.

« Non, nous ne ennuyions pas. Nous nous sommes beaucoup amusés, nous avons fait beaucoup de jeux. Oui, bien sûr, les jeux étaient très différents, nous n'avions pas d'ordinateurs, de télé ou de téléphone. Nous inventions des histoires, nous chantions et dansions, nous montions des pièces de théâtre pour nos parents. En hiver, nous patinions sur la rivière gelée et nous faisions de la luge dans la neige. Mon enfance a été très occupée ; les enfants devaient aider leurs parents mais nous avions aussi le temps de jouer. Nous faisions beaucoup de jouets nous-mêmes, nous utilisions notre imagination ! »

« Invente une histoire, Grand-mère ! ».

« Voyons voir, regarde par la fenêtre, qu'est-ce que tu vois? »

« Rien du tout », répond Theo.

« Moi, je vois une étoile » dit Isabelle.

« Moi aussi », dit Grand-mère. « Elle est loin, mais on peut la voir dans un nombre de pays différents. »

« Est-ce qu'on peut jouer une pièce, Grand-mère ? »

« Pourquoi pas. D'abord, il faut décider d'un thème. »

« Pourquoi pas dans les montagnes d'Ecosse ? Sans ordinateur. Faire semblant d'être poursuivis par des monstres dans la neige. Recherchons des vieux vêtements dans l'armoire de Maman et Papa ! ».

Les enfants se sont bien amusés dans ce monde différent. Le spectacle a bien sûr eu lieu aux chandelles, sous les applaudissements des spectateurs. Ce soir-là, les enfants ont bien apprécié leur histoire au coucher. Et ils ont rêvé des montagnes distantes de notre veille Ecosse.

« Et bien, Maman, as-tu aimé ta visite dans le passé ? »

« Tu sais que j'adore ça. Et les enfants aussi. C'était un monde différent à l'époque. »

A ce moment-là, Paul entre avec des boissons. « Je crois que tu mérites un petit dram, Grand-mère. Et moi aussi » conclut-il. Slainte!

Ellen's home language is English.

鹳, 回去你的土地

Malwina Ciecielag

Once upon a time, there lived a stork that decided to emigrate to more abundant lands. When he finally reached his destination, he came across an eagle ...

"你为什么来这里?" Eagle snorted dryly.

"你好!" Said Stork.

"我的家有八口鹳。"

"我来为家人寻找食物。 你有很多食物， 你的土地物产很丰富。"

"你为什么不友好?"

"我不是外星人。"

"我对这个世界很好奇!" Explained stork.

"我们的北方很有钱，也很漂亮。" Bragged eagle.

Eagle warned how many conditions must be met:

"你必须适应。 你能说我们的语言吗? 你看小说吗?" Questioned Eagle.

"要留在这儿，你必须证明自己是一个英雄，去拯救某个人，或者做一件不一般的事。" Eagle's conditions were unbearable ...

"什么意思?" Asked Stork.

"我是你们中的一员 ......'

"回到你的土地去。" Eagle grumbled.

The stork saddened. He thought:

"我不有名，不强大，也不勇敢......"

The stork was an average bird and could not do anything extraordinary.

Suddenly, out of nowhere, a phoenix appeared. He was beautiful and majestic and spoke all of the languages.

"鹰，什么都不要说了! 你为什么生气?"

Then, he turned to stork;

"你好！我的朋友。见到你，我很高兴。你为什么想离开你的土地？"

"你高兴吗？"Asked Phoenix .

"不太高兴......我应该不应该回去?" Replied Stork.

"我邀请你到我的世界来。" Said Phoenix.

"In our different world there is only one rule: To be kind to each other".

He rose to the sky and solemnly recited:

"Nikt nie podbija nowych ziem, ponieważ jesteśmy zadowoleni z tego, co mamy. Chciwość i zazdrość jest nam obca. Nie oceniamy innych i pomagamy wszystkim w potrzebie. Doceniamy każdy dzień i jego prostotę. Podziwiamy wschodzące słońce, krople rosy na trawie, radujemy się smakiem dojrzałych wiśni, a najbardziej doceniamy możliwość wstawania każdego ranka przy boku naszych najbliższych. Żyjemy tu i teraz...

Welcome to our new, different world ..."

"是另一个世界, 我一直向往的世界......" Stork sighed deeply...

And what world would you like to live in? The choice is so obvious...

一路平安

Malwina's home language is Polish.

Over the rainbow

Tosia Altman

We would speak about this time years later, with an odd sort of fondness and longing, from when the world slowed and stopped spinning on its axel.

We would remember a time when neighbours wouldn't just nod at each other, but instead would dance and clap together outside on the chalk drawings on the pavements, the pastel rainbows shining up at us, as we felt the sacrifices that people had made so we could stand there.

With the world slowed and the shops closed, we learnt to enjoy the quiet days, playing games from our childhood, with old tennis rackets, skipping ropes and bikes being rediscovered from the garage where they had long taken up residence, as new sets of legs found the joys of simple living.

But it was also a time when people would look at each in empathy knowing that each of us would have lost something from the silent disease that made the 2m distance between us into a heavy reminder. Our children would clutch at our legs, holding their arms up beseechingly, as we prayed for those who we couldn't feel but could see, as we looked at our parents and grandparents through the window pane, praying they would walk to the end of the tunnel with us.

Then we would bend and lift, proffering our child to the window, as innocent hands reached out to press against the weathered one, despite the barrier. Then the yearning to be able to hug or kiss them would grow until it became an aching agony as we looked at each other.

Our little ones would look at us, with the most beautiful of eyes, and would ask with a trembling lip, *'Why? Why can't I hug babcia?'* as we held them to us, grateful for the small mercy of being able to do that.

But eventually the world began to gradually spin again, and we finally saw our children hugging their *babcia* as we smiled at the neighbours, holding our hands and arms out to each other, free of masks and gloves, as we moved to embrace at last.

Tosia's home language is English.

Body Language

Adele Guyton

Le 54e jour, j'ouvre ma porte, je quitte ma chambre, je vais au parc parce que les bancs sont ouverts à nouveau. Celui au bord du bois est le lieu de notre rencontre. Quelque chose m'attend quand j'arrive, un truc
    des mots
    ils . . sont
    empilés, la
    forme
    d'une
    femme
    qui est
    / assise sur
    / un   banc
    / au   bord
    / du   bois vert,
    / mon banc préféré
    / ou je...........cherche
    /   mon
    /   amie
    /   ce
    /   truc
    /   dit : : : : :
« Bist du das ? »

Je dis que je ne comprends pas. Je dis que je vais essayer en anglais.

« What did you say ? »

La chose, la femme, mon amie ? Elle dit : « Ich verstehe dich nicht », dans une langue que je ne connais pas.

« Wait a moment. » Je prends mon portable de ma poche. J'écris : « Tu es la femme sur le banc ? Je ne te comprends pas ! »

Il y a le son de sa sonnerie. Mon SMS a été envoyé. Deux paroles sur son visage s'approchent.

Les deux mots, sont-ils ses sourcils ? Est-ce qu'elle est perplexe ?

« I can't read you » je dis. « Can you read me ? » Parce-que je peux voir les mots mais pas son visage.

Un coup de fil dans ma main : « Oui, c'est moi ! Qu'est-ce-que tu as fait avec ton corps pendant le confinement ?! »

Je m'assieds à son côté. « C'est bizarre de te voir comme ça » je dis, et je mime l'action d'être au téléphone. « Appelle-moi ? »

Elle comprend.

Mon oreille gauche:
« Häh, wir haben uns doch per Skype so gut verstanden !
Was soll der Scheiß, ich erkenne dich gar nicht mehr wieder! »

* * *

Mon oreille droite, où je tiens mon portable:
« C'est quoi ça, nous nous sommes entendus très
bien sur Skype, non ? Putain, je ne te reconnais pas… »

Adele's home language is English.

La nueva normalidad

Steven Johnstone

Ya lo había visto todo antes el molusco. En este planeta y en los anteriores; ellos, los humanos, lo habían estropeado todo. Una vez verde, con agua limpia y aire fresco, el mundo se había convertido en un lugar seco, sucio, donde una cosa llamada dinero, parecía ser más importante que casi todo lo demás. El molusco planeaba irse - una nueva vida en un nuevo planeta.

Pero hoy, todo parecía diferente. El molusco podía ver el cielo, azul y brillante, libre de los miles de aviones, tan comunes antes. Olía las flores en lugar del fuego y la contaminación. Oía los pájaros cantando en los árboles previamente ocultos por edificios y hormigón. Los ríos y los mares corrían con el agua nuevamente clara. El mundo parecía más brillante, más vibrante, a pesar de, o quizás a causa de, una falta de personas. Quizás no lo había visto todo antes, el molusco.

—¿Qué pasa? —se preguntó a sí mismo, disfrutando de la soledad.

—Se han despertado —respondió una voz.

En ese momento, apareció un erizo. Continuó explicando:

—Ha llegado al mundo algo serio. Invisible, pero muy serio, y de lo que todo el mundo comenta como nunca antes.

—¿Quién eres? —preguntó el molusco.

Pero el erizo no pausó ni para presentarse ni para respirar.

—Tiene un impacto horrible. Pasa por todo el mundo matando

humanos y destruyendo el estilo de vida tan querido entre los del poder, los del dinero. ¿Has oído hablar del dinero? Es algo muy raro…

—Basta ya… —interrumpió otra voz, esta de una abeja, sentándose en una flor cercana—. Lo que necesitáis saber es que los humanos parecen haber cambiado. Se hablan, comen juntos, no siempre tienen prisa y, escuchad esto: ¡aún parecen felices!

El molusco estaba atónito:

—No he visto esto antes —dijo él—. Tal vez me quede aquí al fin.

A partir de ese día, los tres se hicieron amigos y cada vez se les unían más, prosperando en este nuevo mundo limpio, equilibrado y amistoso. Había fiestas en las selvas y los bosques, más ruidos y colores de los que jamás hubieran imaginado y con un tipo de vida que no habían visto nunca. ¿Y los humanos? Seguían siendo más felices, más tranquilos, sin tantas preocupaciones y con más tiempo. Respetaban el entorno natural y vivían una vida más sencilla.

—Este debe ser otro planeta —opinó el molusco—. Si no fuese así, ¿debe ser un sueño?

—No, —dijo la abeja— esta es la nueva normalidad. Tenemos otra oportunidad y esta vez vamos a hacerlo bien.

Steven's home language is English.

A sudden sense of precariousness

Antonella Matellicani

I wish I could have had some thoughtless time and positive energy during those bleak early days, when nobody cared much to see the light of a new day outside or the smiley faces of neighbours that normally say 'Buongiorno'. In those days no thought that wasn't horrific or tragic crossed my mind and probably, if I could have had more members of my family around me I wouldn't have been able to feel any happier anyway, as I would have seen and suffered, daily, fear and anxiety overwhelming the hearts of the people I love.

Every day on the phone with my mum asking me: "Come stai, tutto bene?" at least three times a day to make sure she wouldn't feel that sense of emptiness that, by contrast, was filling my entire daily routine. Elderly people are the ones at bigger risk, I thought; they keep on saying this on the telly. But when I spoke to my mum, I had to forget about the catastrophic headlines coming from the TV. How painful it was for me to try and not sound worried. She said to me: "Non ce la faccio più! Hai sentito quante migliaia di persone in terapia intensiva?". Of course I had heard that hundreds had entered intensive care but je devais être forte, comme dit mon étudiante française Corinne. Il ne faut pas lui montrer (my mother) que tu t'inquiètes pour elle, elle continue. Malheureusement les parents qui ne sont plus jeunes et ont d'autres problèmes de santé sont les plus à risque.

Merci bien Corinne ! I thought, merci de chercher à me peindre la réalité telle qu'elle est, si tu veux, à me rapporter à des millions d'autres gens qui souffrent ma même condition, celle d'une femme adulte abasourdie par la peur de perdre la seule personne qui, que cela me plaise ou non, vivra dans tous mes jours futurs.

Every day, from breakfast to bedtime, I kept on swallowing medical, statistical and bulletin-like notions that were spoken by broken-voiced journalists, whose frightened eyes were the only thing exposed. Una situazione assurda, dolorosa e surreale dalla quale si vuole uscire al più presto e che si vuole cancellare, come si cancella un brutto incubo.

In those days you realised how little and vulnerable you are.

The *WhatsApp* group I was asked to be part of was set up at a party, by an all-time group of friends just one week before the dark threat fell and squashed our lives. How blissful those posts were, telling of the good time we had enjoyed! They looked, however, so anachronistic to me and terribly irresponsible. "Scusate se ho paura", I said to them, "nascondere la testa sotto la sabbia e negare la gravità della situazione è da incoscienti". The bliss was nowhere to be seen and I told them. We were being 'invaded and attacked' by an unknown micro-killer and these folks posted *YouTube* music on *WhatsApp*?!

I simply laid myself bare, I suddenly grew older and knew a new 'me'. I was privileged.

Antonella's home language is Italian.

Unas vacaciones de ensueño

Rachel Evans

Esta es la historia de dos hermanas, Eva y Elise, que sueñan con los tiempos de cuando tenían aventuras emocionantes explorando países diferentes.

—¿Recuerdas cuando fuimos a Tailandia? —preguntó Elise—. Me encantaron esas vacaciones. ¡Ojalá que podamos ir otra vez!

—¡Elise, cállate, mañana tenemos un día ocupado con lecciones, se tiene que dormir! —dijo Eva.

«Más lecciones», pensó Elise. Elise se acostó en su cama, pensando en los lugares que le gustaría visitar: Japón con los templos y pagodas, China con los rascacielos o Brasil con el Carnaval. «¡O quizás iré al espacio!» siguió pensando Elise cerrando sus ojos.

—¡Elise! —gritó Eva—. ¡Date prisa! El autobús a Tokio llega en cinco minutos.

Su primera escala fue el Palacio Imperial, el hogar de la Familia Imperial desde 1457. Los jardines eran bonitos y tranquilos con estanques, carpas y una casa de té tradicional. Próxima escala, Ginza, el distrito famoso de Tokio y el japonés corazón de la moda. Finalmente, al final del día, Temboin con un mercado con comida deliciosa y vistas de las pagodas.

—Siempre he querido ver una pagoda japonesa —dijo Eva—. ¿Podemos mirar?

—Sí, iremos por la puerta de delante y saldremos por el lado. ¡Quítate los zapatos y no hables! —Elise susurró.

Las chicas entraron al templo, había una gran estatua de Buda y gente rezando. Se dieron la vuelta y se fueron silenciosamente. Pero, cuando salieron, la vista era diferente. Estaban en frente de un río ancho con veleros y al otro lado del río, rascacielos iluminados fantásticos.

El área estaba llena de gente caminando y en la distancia podían ver una torre alta con esferas brillantes y una antena opulenta en la parte superior: la Torre de la Perla Oriental, un símbolo famoso de Shanghái.

—Elise, es el Bund y el río Yangtsé, ¡estamos en China!

Las chicas caminaron, admirando los rascacielos modernos y la gente practicando Tai Chi. ¡Qué asombroso!

—Debemos ir a Nanjing Road con millones de tiendas —dijo Eva.

Después de ir de compras, las chicas fueron al río para ir en un viaje en barco. Compraron sus billetes y subieron. ¡El barco navegó por el río y las chicas vieron loros y tucanes en los árboles y tenían mucho calor!

—Elise, que raro, ¿esto no es China? ¡estamos en una selva tropical!

En la distancia, las chicas oyeron el sonido de Samba.

—¡Estamos en Brasil! —dijo Eva.

Pudieron ver el Cristo Redentor en la cima de la montaña Corcovado, la estatua más famosa de Brasil y una de las siete maravillas del mundo.

—¡Río de Janeiro! ¡Estamos en Río! —gritó Elise.

Desde el barco, las chicas vieron bailar la samba, admirando los disfraces y las carrozas coloridas mientras bebían una caipiriña.

—Eva, me encanta Brasil y me encantan estas vacaciones.

—Y a mí también. Pero, ahora estoy cansada, necesito dormir.

Y Elise cerró sus ojos.

—¡Eva despierta! ¡Debemos levantarnos, tenemos una lección!

«Pues» pensó Elise, «¡estoy en mi casa después de mis vacaciones de ensueño!».

Rachel's home language is English.

Musically speaking

Tamsin Morris

'Je préfère les plantes.'

'Sí, porque estás loco.'

Alex snorted. 'And that's a surprise? He's stuck in a chateau, with 60 musicians. He hasn't been out for eight weeks. And, most importantly, he's a viola player, he's French and he's playing with a Spanish orchestra. Of course he's mad and of course he prefers the plants'

Yves shook his head and turned away. 'Je préfère les plantes, les arbres, les oiseaux. Ils sont un public très raffiné. Ils ne toussent pas, ils ne mangent pas. Ils écoutent. Et je crois qu'ils sont l'avenir. Pour moi, c'est l'avenir.'

'Sí, es verdad. Escuchan. Pero, las aves no pagan. Entonces, no es el futuro. O, si es el futuro, no es un futuro para nosotros. ¿Entiendes?' Juan was always less tolerant than the other musicians. He was a brass player – used to being the centre of attention with a strident viewpoint.

Alex nodded. 'I agree. We can't live here forever. It's bad enough that we got stuck here in this lockdown, confinement, call it what you will. But we can't stop playing concerts. At some point, we'll have to go back into the big, bad world and hope that people haven't forgotten how to listen. It's been lovely playing together in the courtyard, but we can't make money playing to the trees and a handful of scruffy birds that might choose to flit through. You'll need to face the world again one day, Yves.'

Four months later, the Argentinean National Orchestra finally made it home. Their tour of Europe had the misfortune to coincide with a global pandemic, leading to a multinational group of highly strung musicians spending four months in a French château, waiting out the shutdown. To pass the time, they'd rehearsed in the castle grounds, with a dedicated following of house plants carefully stationed in the seats they'd put out to remind them of the audience. When they finally escaped on a plane to Buenos Aires, they celebrated their return by playing their first public concert to national acclaim.

As the audience shuffled out, Alex dropped his violin back in its case. 'Well. That was tough.'

'Sí, sí, sí.' Juan wiped his sweaty face. 'La gente. Uf. Increíble. Ellos no escuchan. Charla, charla, charla. Tos, tos, tos. Ahora, prefiero las plantas también.'

'J'ai une idée.' Yves looked, if anything, even sweatier and more depressed than the others. 'Nous rentrons en France. Au château. Et nous jouerons seulement pour les plantes. Je n'aime pas l'argent. Je n'aime pas le monde maintenant. J'aime le silence.'

'¿Y la paz? ¿Y la camaradería? Sí. Yo también. Ahora, es un mundo nuevo. Y yo prefiero el mundo de confinamiento. Regresamos ahora.'

Alex sighed. 'I wish it were possible. I liked that world too. Just us and the music and the lovely quiet plants. I wish we could return. But it's a different world now.'

Tamsin's home language is English.

Mon voyage au temps passé

Mackenzie Craig

Un jour en 2020, j'ai acheté un livre sur les années 1970 dans une brocante locale. J'étais enfant alors, et il m'a rappelé des événements, mes rêves, mes désirs et mes expériences. Cependant, je n'étais pas très heureuse, car il y avait cinq enfants dans ma famile (j'étais la troisième) et je devais toujours partager une chambre avec mes frères et soeurs. Naturellement, j'étais jalouse de chaque enfant qui possédait sa propre chambre. Mes cheveux était mi-longs. J'adorais les chevaux, les bijoux en argent, les sacs en cuir avec des bretelles et des chaînes, et la musique pop de façon obsessionnelle, ce qui ennuyait souvent ma famille!

Après avoir commencé à le lire, je me suis endormie. Puis, un brouillard épais m'a entourée. Lorsqu'il s'est éclairci, je me suis retrouvée à cette époque, une jeune femme! Je portais encore les mêmes bijoux en argent, j'avais le même sac en cuir, mais cette fois je portais un pantalon évasé et un T-shirt ample. En plus, mes cheveux étaient très longs et bouclés, comme je les voulais.

J'avais passé huit O-levels, et je faisais mes études d'infirmière. En conséquence, je pouvais aller aux célèbres courses du Grand National, manger au restaurant et danser dans les boîtes de nuit. J'ai vu le cheval Red Rum gagner cette course trois fois. On a pris une photo de moi l'acclamant en 1974 et 1977. Je l'ai même monté une fois à Southport! Et là, j'ai encore vu ma photo dans les journaux!

Les discothèques étaient populaires. Je visitais des lieux tels que

Thackerays et Deep. On mangeait fréquemment à L'Horizon, au Gruchy, au Royal Yacht, au France et aussi à L'escargot à l'hôtel Ambassadeur.

De plus, grâce à mon indépendence, je pouvais aller aux concerts de musique. Imaginez ma grande joie de rencontrer mon groupe favori, Abba. J'ai aussi vu Gary Glitter deux fois, en portant mon propre ensemble scintillant. Quels jours heureux! Puis, en 1978, je suis allée à Wimbledon pour regarder la finale de tennis entre Björn Borg et Jimmy Connors. J'étais engouée des deux joueurs, surtout quand ils m'ont embrassée et m'ont donné leur autographe.

J'adorais aussi les vêtements. Les maisons de couture Gemini, Briggs et Gearbox étaient très populaires. Il y avait un solde chez Gemini. J'y ai acheté un pantalon bleu marine et un T-shirt bleu avec un motif floral. J'ai aussi acheté des sacs en cuir.

Soudain, une brume épaisse a tournoyé sinistrement partout. Je ne pouvais rien voir; j'étais terrifiée! Cinq minutes plus tard, elle a disparu. J'ai entendu mon nouveau portable émettre un bip, et j'étais retournée à 2020. J'ai raconté mon expérience sensationelle à tout le monde. « Oh, tu me moques, a gloussé mon amie Clare, tu étais trop jeune ! »

Mais quand je lui ai montré les photos, les autographes et les programmes du Grand National des années 70, elle a bien dû me croire!

Mackenzie Craig's home language is English.

Apenas un soplo de aire

Daysy Rodríguez

De pronto sentí como un escalofrío nauseabundo que recorría todo mi cuerpo, el cual no podía controlar. No, no era como los de siempre que se sienten cuando tienes gripe, fiebre, y simplemente te tomas algo como un vaso de leche caliente con miel, como solían decirte las abuelas, y pasas la noche y al día siguiente te sientes como nuevo. ¡Y ya está!

¡De pronto todo me daba vueltas! Sudaba. Un sudor frío.

El pecho estaba encogiéndose por momentos, como si una fuerte mano lo estuviera estrujando con todas sus ganas, como si me lo estuvieran arrancando del cuerpo.

«¡Qué dolor! ¡Qué sufrimiento tan intenso!» Era indescriptible… ahora que lo pienso.

«¡Qué desgracia! Ese vacío que se siente, ese dolor perpetuo que jamás te abandona».

¡Tan intenso! Que se arraiga y te maltrata.

Y lo peor de todo, esa sustancia gaseosa, transparente, inodora e insípida, me faltaba. No podía respirar, creo.

El aire se había vuelto espeso, tan denso que parecía estar tragando algo parecido a la *Maizena* que preparaba mi madre cuando era pequeña para desayunar cuando no quería comer a penas. Pero ni eso siquiera podía tragar. Se me atragantaba, se me hacían grumos que a media garganta parecían establecerse allí y no continuaban ni para arriba, ni para abajo. Burbujas enormes atascadas en las tuberías de mis engranajes.

«¡Era una sensación tan desagradable que ni al diablo se la recomendaría yo, como sería ella!»

Y de pronto me di cuenta de que no estaba en mi habitación, ni en mi casa, ni con mi pijama de siempre. Llevaba una especie de camisón azul claro sin botones y unas medias verdes hasta las rodillas que apretaban como los chorizos del pueblo de mi abuela en tiempos aquellos de matanza en Asturias, chorizos embutidos a más no poder a presión por las ancianas del lugar y colgados de los balcones hasta secarse.

¡Y no notaba si llevaba ropa interior! ¡Dios mío qué vergüenza! Quién me viera ahora… ¿Qué diría mi madre? ¡Y qué pensaría mi abuela, que en paz descanse!

¿Y qué es eso que me cuelga de todas partes? ¡Una especie de cables y tubos que van de un lado a otro de mi cama y…

¡Oh, my God! Me acabo de dar cuenta de dónde me hallo.

Estoy en el hospital. ¿Y yo qué hago aquí entre tanta parafernalia? Apenas recuerdo que estaba en casa con mi hijo jugando a un juego nuevo que tiene y que aún no comprendo cómo es capaz de concentrarse tanto. Estos jóvenes de ahora, ¡qué destreza tienen con las nuevas tecnologías!

¿Será que me estoy haciendo mayor?, que no «vieja» como algunos de ellos imploran. Porque yo pienso que la edad es apenas un mero número y que la importancia o no de la edad está en la mentalidad que cada uno tiene.

Y ¿qué importancia ha de tener una arruga más o menos, cuando no te queda un soplo de aire para decir las cosas que más importan a las personas que más amas?

¡Dios mío! ¿Quién eres tú? ¿Acaso un ángel del futuro vestido con bata fría y mascarilla, «irreconocible» con un parapeto de plástico sobre tu cara? ¿Han de ser así los últimos momentos de mi vida? ¿Cierto?

Y entonces le dije como bien pude:

—Por favor, recuérdale a ése a quien tanto quiero, que aunque ya no esté aquí, jamás estaré lejos de su corazón, como le contaba de niño en aquel cuento.

Daysy's home language is Spanish.

A fox's tail

Stefanie Ramcke

'Damned weatherthingi, internetz' gone, no internetz, no series,' she
sighed.

'Thunderstorm, Rita, not weatherthingi,' Tom corrected,
grinning.

'Ja, ja,' Rita replied, 'and you don't know what *that* means.'

'I always thought that meant "yes".' He looked really confused.

'Among other things,' Rita smiled cunningly. 'I'm sorry, this day
was just an awful mess.'

'Until now.' Tom kissed her.

'I really need a few minutes to turn off, switch off my brain, send
my mind out on a trip. Can't you make up a little story, I love your
stories.'

'Okay,' he said and giggled softly, 'Let's see if I can turn you off'.
Tom stretched and paused for a moment 'I will tell you about a fox,
that whipped his tail as it ran through the snow, and you will see…
Let's go for a walk.'

He closed his eyes.

'The woods far up in the polar north smell different, you know.'
His voice gently flew through the room like a current of light and
sound.

'What do they smell like?'

'Walk with me.' His words purled, 'I can hear the sound of our
steps. An auspicious breeze carries it far into the woods and heralds

our arrival. A hint of chill is in the air, tenaciously pronouncing the winter at our doorstep. But today, bright yellow and orange colours of birches shine through the pines and a myriad of single red berries on a tiny twig cover the ground. So peaceful and silent. Oh look, the sun is already going down.

The pines. You know the beautiful aroma of pines. The first wafts of mist feature the scent of the damp forest floor, wilderness and decay. But there is something else. There is wood smoke in the air. Like a bonfire but gentle and soft. See that twig? Pick it up. It looks grey and weathered, take a deep breath, smell the incense.

We move along in the last light of the day. Step by step, steady and slowly into the darkness. There is the lake, and the old schoolhouse. But look up, you're looking in the wrong direction! See there? Pillars of purple and pink. And above, white cloudlike swirls pulsating slowly like a breath, and now a massive bright green Lindworm manifests itself out of the blue, meanders over our heads, its dragonlike spikes reach down to us, pulses of light flash through it. It fills up all the night sky. See how the upper ends turn to pink, look, there comes another one. Stagnates, then moves again, disappears and comes back in a flash. Slowly but steadily the bright lights start to fade and the cold polar night returns. It's warm inside, wanna go in?' Tom recalls her.

'Aber du hast noch gar nichts über den Fuchs erzählt,' Rita murmured.

'The fox?' Tom smiled. 'The fox whips up snow crystals with its tail on its journey through the polar forests. They fly all the way high up into the sky, hence the bright lights, that's what the Sami people say. And they must know, they have lived here forever.'

Stefanie's home language is German.

· Day ten ·

Lluna

Debi Barry

Hoy es el día.

A medida que se acerca a la puerta de la sala del hospital, las imágenes de días monótonos, días decepcionantes, vuelven a aparecer. ¿Será este diferente? Quizás. Esperanza siente como un leve destello de esperanza se alza dentro de ella. Ella lo aprovecha, desterrando los pensamientos de fracaso a los rincones más oscuros de su mente. Le da un empujón a la puerta; su obstinada resistencia simboliza el desafío que se avecina. «Hoy será diferente», promete. Su elección de idioma ya está hecha: español.

—¡Buenos días Lluna! —dijo ella susurrando.

Busca un parpadeo del "paciente", el movimiento de un dedo, alguna cosa, cualquier cosa.

Nada.

—¿Cómo está hoy mi pequeña? ¿Quieres algo para desayunar? —dice sonriendo.

El pitido del monitor de frecuencia cardíaca es el único sonido que rompe el silencio.

Esperanza se desploma en la silla de visitante y estudia la cara de la niña. Después de tantas visitas, tantas horas, ella conoce cada línea, cada curva. Su largo cabello rubio se desplegaba detrás de ella, iluminando su rostro como si una cerilla iluminara una habitación oscura. ¡Qué apropiado que se llamara Lluna! Esperanza reflexiona, significa "luna" en castellano y era la única pista de la identidad de la niña.

Lluna había sido encontrada a medianoche fuera de la entrada principal del hospital. Los niños abandonados siempre despiertan el interés de los medios. Éste no fue diferente, solo que esta vez, nadie se presentó. Nadie llamó. La policía, habiendo agotado todas las líneas de investigación, se dio por vencida y la abandonó por segunda vez. O eso sentía Esperanza. Se prometió a sí misma que no abandonaría a la niña.

Desentrañar el origen étnico de Lluna se había convertido en un enigma que Esperanza personalmente tenía que resolver. Descubrir su lengua materna, devolverla a la conciencia, podría resolver el rompecabezas de su vida. Dada la pálida apariencia de la niña, Esperanza había comenzado con alemán y francés sin éxito.

—¿Quién eres, Lluna? —volvió a preguntar— ¿De dónde diablos vienes? —Se frotó los ojos con cansancio, su voz temblaba llena de frustración.

Nada.

Aunque era una profesional consumada, sabía que se había apegado a la niña. La falta de progreso la irritaba e hizo que Esperanza se cuestionara sus habilidades: «¿Qué estaba haciendo mal? ¿No era ella una especialista en idiomas muy respetada en su campo?». Ella había ayudado a innumerables niños refugiados a adaptarse a sus nuevos hogares a través del lenguaje. Cada intento fallido con Lluna profundizaba su abatimiento a medida que los meses iban y venían.

—Lluna... ¡por favor! —Su exasperación resonaba por la habitación.

Una enfermera entra a toda prisa en la habitación trayéndola de vuelta al presente.

—¿Algún cambio en nuestra paciente hoy?

«Esperanza era una visitante muy frecuente», bromeaban las enfermeras. Ella se había convertido casi en parte del mobiliario. Esperanza niega con la cabeza con tal desánimo que la enfermera sonríe alentadoramente, y con un encogimiento de hombros afirma:

—Mi abuela solía decir «no perdis mai l'esperança».

Esperanza tarda unos segundos en procesar; aunque entiende catalán, no lo habla.

—On sóc? —La voz crepitante acorta su conversación. Se dan la vuelta. Los ojos de Lluna pasan de Esperanza a la enfermera y viceversa. Confusión. Una ráfaga de palabras se escupe de forma cada vez más incoherente.

—Qui ets? —exige—. No et conec! Vull a la meva mare i al meu pare!

Una pausa. El silencio.

La quietud se rompe en mil pedazos cuando Lluna comienza a gritar.

Debi's home language is English.

Innocent mistakes

Amy Ziemniak

Most people learn some kind of four letter word first when learning new languages. I just didn't know I was saying anything wrong for a very long time until someone was kind enough to point it out to me.

I had married and moved to Germany. My husband, who traveled for work, was only home for two week stretches at the time. Time together was precious so we spoke English for convenience, instead of practicing the German I was learning that was so crucial to my existence. As a result, it was even harder for me to come together with people. Add to that the fact that I was raising my daughter on my own in a country I didn't know and I found I just used whatever language I could to be able to communicate with people. I noticed, every once in a while, that people would look startled, or stare at me open mouthed every so often. I assumed this happened due to my terrible German and that people were just trying to decipher what I had said.

My daughter began to go to kindergarten, seasons changed from spring to summer and it became very warm. There are about two months of unbearable heat in inland Germany, and I did not know how to escape it. Coming from coastal California, I never thought to lower blinds at midday or close doors and windows when it was so nice outside. The result was sweltering and overwhelming. Frankly, I was hot.

I remember having a conversation with another kindergarten mom. It was unbelievably warm that day, and I said, 'Ich bin heiß'. I was trying to strike up a conversation about the weather and how I was suffering from it. I was hot, and I translated it directly. The woman froze and quickly escorted her child out and away from me. I thought it was a bit abrupt, but didn't let it bother me.

Later that summer, I took my daughter to a children's service at the local Catholic church. It was so warm that day, and so gloriously cool inside the old church walls that I welcomed the idea of escaping the heat within. I mentioned it to some other parents saying, 'Ich bin heiß. Ich möchte schnell rein' (I am hot. I want to go in quickly.) They froze, and mentioned they wouldn't keep me from finding my seat. Once again, I thought it strange. No one really talked to me much that day, but then again I was still trying to break into that insider circle.

The rest of the summer went about the same. I tried to talk to people. I told them I was too hot. 'Ich bin sehr heiß' (I am very hot).

November came along and my daughter was invited to a birthday party. This was an age where parents still stayed. It became very warm in the room and I asked if we could open a window, because 'Ich bin heiß'. One of the dads looked at me and said, 'Sag dass nicht' (Don't say that). 'Warum nicht? Ich bin heiß' (Why not? I'm hot) was my reply.

The dad blushed. 'Weil, das bedeutet dass...' (because that means) and he proceeded to very politely explain what I had been saying all along, which was 'I am horny'. Contextually, my direct and innocent translation was embarrassing and slutty. Trying to win friends and come into conversation with people I had been telling them that I was horny. I was very horny. I was horny in the kindergarten, and I was so horny the day I went to church I needed to get inside quickly.

Amy's home language is English.

Le papillon

Pauline Turner

The jumbled letters were there again, sucked into the tiny leaf purses, dangling from the butterfly tree. He could always see the 'j', sometimes an 'e'. They mockingly danced, almost close enough to touch yet just out of reach. Today was no different. He reached out to unfurl the curled up leaves. He reached out to release the letters, to release his tongue. He reached out as the wind whipped them from the trees and they fell, dead and shattered, spitting letters just out of Simon's reach.

Julie woke with a start, still exhausted, and pulled on her jeans from yesterday. It was always the same; the same endless world; the same endless walks; her same endless voice, hushed by her husband's endless silence. She sighed, digging her fists into her pockets. He had deteriorated. She was prepared but not enough: rekindling the last dying embers, extracting those last meaningful words from his world, the world which Julie didn't recognise and where she certainly didn't belong.

The rhythmic beating was in his ears again, his wings. Frantically he searched... *Où est le papillon?* He shook his head. Sweat trickled down his back. He prickled all over as the leaf purses rattled against the wind, spilling their letters in showers of mixed up scrabble around him at the bottom of the tree. He scooped huge handfuls, stuffing as many letters as he could into his satchel, gift wrapping the ones for Julie. *Aujourd'hui est différent. Le papillon est proche.*

It was dusk when Julie arrived at the hospital and the colours were sinking into muted evening tones. She would try his language tonight, their language. The butterfly meadow had been curiously in her mind. He told her that summer that if she placed her wishes on the backs of the butterflies and they flew into the sky, her dreams would come true. Overlooking the Seine, he had helped her to attach many French words and phrases to their wings.

This evening, she held his hand but for once, the tremor was her own. Her voice felt strangely distanced but she had to try this. Taking a deep breath, she stammered « Le papillon vole tes mots, tes rêves, mais moi je vole ton cœur. » His words were too large for her mouth. He had said them so many times that summer. She squeezed his hand and looked for the tiniest light behind his expressionless eyes.

Simon blinked. He had waited for this summer warmth. His heart quickened with the beating wings. Transparent, fluttering colours emerged from the leaf purses, stretching tiny fragile wings. But the letters and words? Where were they? He felt suddenly nauseous, until he remembered. Reaching into his satchel from earlier, he found the words that he had gift wrapped for Julie. Attaching them to the prettiest fluttering colour, the crimson butterfly rose into the late evening, as he smiled...

« Le papillon vole mes mots, mes rêves, mais je te donne mon cœur. »

Pauline's home language is English.

Un 'Celestino', due sconosciuti, tre nazionalità, quattro lingue

Maria Leiva

Angelo, Piemontese, ai sei anni partì per l'Argentina con i suoi genitori. A Córdoba conobbe Rosa e Celestino, i miei carissimi zii... però... io non ero ancora nata... Angelo forse conobbe la mia famiglia al matrimonio di Rosa e Celestino... Dopo otto anni in Argentina, dove fu felice ed imparò a cacciare pernici, andarono in Italia, Africa e dopo, solo per caso, si stabilirono in Inghilterra, ma sempre scambiando notizie con Rosa e Celestino.

A quaranta anni Angelo non aveva ancora trovato la donna giusta. Aveva avuto relazioni, ma quando immaginava la vita insieme dopo dieci anni... lasciava perdere. Voleva una ragazza di famiglia, dell'Argentina, e anche di Córdoba.

Io sono nata a Córdoba e ho sempre studiato l'inglese perché volevo vivere in un paese di lingua inglese, preferibilmente l'Inghilterra... un sogno difficile da realizzare!

Nei miei trentun anni, non ho avuto mai una relazione seria. Anni prima, una carissima amica, Rosana, si era sposata dopo pochi mesi di fidanzamento con Giorgio, un italiano che la adorava! Così, pregai di trovare un italiano che mi amasse così...

A gennaio del 1998 e con l'aiuto e supporto di Silvina – mia sorella – nonché di Víctor (Córdoba), delle carissime famiglie d'Ivette (Stati Uniti) e Sarah (Regno Unito), e dei loro amici, visitai New York e dopo arrivai in Inghilterra il 7 luglio del 1998, con un visto di sei mesi. Così mi avvicinai alla felicità suprema!

Ad ottobre, già ero preoccupata perché dovevo lasciare l'Inghilterra a gennaio!

Zio Celestino scrisse alla famiglia di Angelo: fu così lui ad accendere la prima scintilla di questa storia. Celestino racconta che siccome non eravamo molto lontani l'uno dall'altra, potevamo incontrarci. Così, il sabato 17 ottobre, il mio treno arrivò ad Amersham prima del previsto e scommisi con me stessa, cosi, per gioco, che avrei saputo riconoscere Angelo. Dopo un po', lo vidi passare, però non stava andando in stazione... che strano, pensai. Subito dopo entrò sua madre, con lui dietro, e pregai subito che Angelo fosse single!

Pranzammo ed uscimmo per una passeggiata. Al ritorno, Angelo disse a sua madre: «Lei lu sa ancura nen ma sarà mia fumna...». Il giorno dopo mi portarono a casa e piansi come una bambina quando lui partì...

Dopo esserci visti per due fine settimana, ci fidanzammo! Il mio visto scadeva il 7 gennaio e quindi decidemmo di sposarci prima, per non rischiare!! La mia testa era un mulinello di confusione: in 10 mesi avevo lasciato la mia famiglia dall'altro lato del mondo, vissuto in tre continenti diversi, e ora mi preparavo per sposarmi con uno appena conosciuto! A questo punto, Sarah mi disse: 'Follow your heart!!'

In Argentina, mia sorella Silvina organizzò una festa di "addio al nubilato" per me, nonostante non potessi esserci di persona!! «Chicas, ¡la tesorito de la casa se nos casa! ¿Vienen a la despedida de soltera?»

Silvina venne al matrimonio. Il 2 gennaio 1999 ci sposammo... e 3 anni dopo rimasi incinta. Silvina organizzò una baby shower per me! «Chicas, ¡baby shower para Virgi que está embarazada!»

Nel 2003 nacque José.

Oggi abitiamo a Milton Keynes, con Marcella, la madre di Angelo. Tutti e quattro capiamo quattro lingue: inglese, italiano, spagnolo e anche piemontese.

Chi mai avrebbe immaginato che i sogni così diversi di due persone che non si erano mai viste potessero realizzarsi. E adesso viviamo ancora felici mangiando pernici!

Maria's home language is Spanish.

La conversation du confinement

Julianne McCorry

Facebook Amis: Zoë Lefebvre: invitation envoyée par Claire Comtois

Facebook Amis: Claire Comtois: invitation acceptée par Zoë Lefebvre

Facebook Amis: Zoë Lefebvre: nouveau message de Claire Comtois

Claire: Bonjour Zoë! Comment allez-vous?

Zoë: Bonjour Claire! Je vais bien, merci. Désolée! Je ne reconnais pas votre nom.

Claire: Non, vous ne le reconnaîtrez pas.

Zoë: On s'est déjà rencontrées?

Claire: Non, jamais.

Zoë: On a des amis en commun?

Caire: Non, aucun.

Zoë: Alors…?

Claire: Zoë, j'ai une nouvelle à vous annoncer.

Zoë : Oui? Ça m'a l'air intéressant!

Claire: Je pense que vous feriez mieux de vous asseoir.

Zoë: Pourquoi? De quoi s'agit-il?

Claire: Vous vous êtes assise?

Zoë: Oui! Dites-moi!

Claire: Zoë, je suis votre sœur.

Zoë: Quoi? Qu'est-ce que vous voulez dire?

Claire: Je suis votre sœur. Pour être précis, votre demi-sœur.

Zoë: *silence*

Claire: Zoë? Désolée, je sais que c'est un vrai choc. Je n'avais pas d'autre moyen de vous contacter.

Zoë: Comment pouvez-vous être ma sœur? C'est impossible. Je suis fille unique.

Claire: Ça fait longtemps……

Zoë: Mes parents se sont mariés très jeunes, et mon père n'était pas du genre infidèle. Il ne pouvait pas être votre père. C'est ridicule! Que voulez-vous?

Claire: Zoë, il ne s'agit pas de votre père. Votre mère a eu un bébé quand elle était ado. Le bébé a été adopté.

Zoë: Quoi???

Claire: Le bébé, c'était moi.

Zoe: Comment pouvez-vous le savoir?

Claire: Après la mort de mes parents adoptifs, j'ai fait des recherches, et je suis tombée sur le nom de ma mère biologique. Elle s'appelait Catherine Dubois.

Zoë: Le nom de ma mère, vraiment, mais sans aucun doute, une personne différente. C'est une pure coïncidence. Adieu, Claire!

Claire: Zoë, bref, vous vous rappelez que vous vous êtes inscrite sur le site web généalogique, Geneanet? Comme moi, vous y avez déposé vos données ADN?

Zoë: Oui. Il y a deux mois, pendant le confinement, quand je n'avais pas grand-chose à faire. Pour faire des recherches sur mes ancêtres. Pourquoi?

Claire: La semaine dernière, j'ai reçu une alerte de Geneanet. Nous sommes un match! Nous avons 27% d'ADN partagé. Ça correspond à une relation demi-fraternelle. Les résultats sont incontestables. Vous pouvez le vérifier vous-même sur le site web.

Zoë: Je suis en train de me connecter. Ah. J'ai aussi une alerte. C'est incroyable.

Claire: Zoë, je suis ravie de vous avoir trouvée…

Zoë: J'ai besoin d'un verre! Mais ma mère est morte. Je ne peux pas lui demander…

Claire: Oui, je sais. C'est dommage. J'aurais aimé faire sa connaissance.

Zoë: Qui était votre père?

Claire: Tristement, je doute que je ne saurai jamais.

Zoe: Vous avez quel âge?
Claire: 50 ans. Vous?
Zoë: 45. Pouvez-vous poster une photo?
Claire: Oui - en voilà une.
Zoë: Mon Dieu! Ma mère, vous lui ressemblez beaucoup. Moi aussi. C'est donc bien vrai. Vous habitez où? En France?
Claire: Oui, à Bordeaux.
Zoë: Bordeaux? Quel quartier?
Claire: Chartrons. Vous connaissez?
Zoë: Quelle rue?
Claire: rue du Maréchal Foch.
Zoë: Quel numéro?
Claire: 29. ???
Zoë: Attendez! J'arrive dans deux minutes…

Julianne's home language is English.

New life

Luis Garcia Sanchez

Bruno was born in Malaga, in Spain, at the end of the sixties, and moved to Dundee in Scotland in the winter of 2013. This is his story...

In Spain, he used to work as a Spanish/English interpreter for the government, and had his own restaurant with quite a few people working for him. But because of the economic crisis, from 2010 he started to suffer economically and finally went bankrupt by the end of 2012 around Christmas time. And as they say in Spain, 'when the money doesn't come through the door, love leaves through the window.' So, one thing followed the other and after bankruptcy came divorce.

Bruno had two options: to stay in bed crying and feeling sorry for himself, or try to fight for a new future for himself and his 3 children. Of course, he chose the second option and decided to leave the country and start all over again somewhere else where the economy was better. He tried to go to the USA or Canada because he had friends over there and had lived and worked over there before, but by that time it was difficult to get a visa, so some friends who lived in Dundee invited Bruno to come over and stay with them until he could move on and manage by himself. So that is what he did. In January 2013, he moved to Dundee and from March of that same year he has worked every single day without any gap. His first job was in a car body workshop and then he worked in a

Mexican restaurant in St. Andrews and finally as a full-time supervisor in a hotel at the same time as he was working part time as a taxi driver.

The following year, Bruno brought his two oldest teenagers over to live with him. Between his jobs and coping with single fatherhood, he was going crazy, so he decided to study and keep his mind busy with something new.

After a while, Bruno chose to study Modern Languages to eventually become a Spanish teacher because he enjoyed teaching and that would be a massive improvement in his professional life. He is now incredibly happy and says that finding the Open University was one of the best things that could have happened to him.

It wasn't easy – nobody gives you anything for free in this life – but Bruno knows it was worth fighting for what he believed and it made him feel alive and able to do whatever he set as his goal. Learning something new is an amazing opportunity for change. There are no limits if you believe in yourself.

Luis' home language is Spanish.

El confinamiento de Pablo

Paula Tompkins Lofty

Me llamo Pablo y vivo con la familia Jiménez en Inglaterra. Somos cinco. Dolores y Pedro los padres, Miguel y María los hijos, y por supuesto, yo soy el perro. Es el mes de junio, 2020. ¿Qué pienso del confinamiento? Bueno, he tenido que vivir con una familia muy frustrada. Quedarse en casa es muy difícil para una familia que ama salir y ser sociable. Pedro está trabajando desde casa, Dolores sigue trabajando como enfermera. Miguel suele ir a la universidad, pero no ahora. Siempre hace ruido con su coche. Cada vez que pone el pie en el acelerador, tengo que ladrar. Luego, me dice que me calle. María, normalmente va a la escuela secundaria, pero ahora, no es muy feliz. No está permitido visitar a amigos o familiares fuera de la casa.

En marzo y abril los perros sólo podían ir a dar un paseo una vez al día con sus dueños. Tenía demasiada energía, y perseguía a los pájaros en el jardín. Un día, me dio un paseo María. Fuimos al parque y conocimos a tres de sus amigos: dos chicos y una chica. Uno de los chicos le besó en la mejilla. Me sorprendió, y mis dueños estaban muy enojados cuando nos vieron. Nos ordenaron que nos metiéramos en el coche y Pedro condujo a casa. Creo que Pedro estaba aún más enojado porque quería ver el fútbol en la televisión, a pesar de que era un partido viejo.

Pues esta es mi familia. Tenemos vecinos a cada lado de nosotros. A un lado, hay una familia francesa. Tienen una gata que se llama Fifi. El otro día Fifi estuvo en nuestro jardín, así que salí y la perseguí. Saltó sobre la valla y luego saltó a la pared que se encuentra en el fondo de su jardín. Me miró y me dijo en francés:

—Bonjour, Monsieur Chien. Comment ça se passe pour vous ? Moi, ça va très bien. Les chats peuvent sortir tous les jours et quand nous le voulons. Je suis très désolé pour vous.

En ese momento me enfadé mucho, así que gruñí y le ladré, pero me ignoró y se fue.

Para ser honesto, estoy un poco celoso de Fifi. Sin embargo, unas semanas después de nuestro encuentro en el jardín, se rompió la pata, y ha tenido que quedarse en la casa durante las últimas seis semanas. Sé que a veces me enoja, Fifi, pero estoy muy feliz de saber que se está recuperando.

Los vecinos del otro lado son italianos y tienen un loro que no para de hablar. A veces se sienta fuera en su jaula. Me gustaría callarlo. A Fifi también, pero cada vez que está cerca de la jaula, el loro grita y la señora sale y grita también:

—Vai via, gatto cattivo. Lascia stare Pavarotti. Povero, Pavarotti —dice la señora.

—Sono un bel ragazzo —dice el loro.

Sí, para un perro ha sido muy difícil el confinamiento, pero la heroína para mi es Dolores, la enfermera, y cada día espero con ansia que ella vuelva a casa.

Paula's home language is English.

Morgen geht's dir besser

Jean Williams

Es war trocken, als Katy das Terrassenhaus verließ. Sie winkte Rhodri, der sie durch das Fenster beobachtete. Sie sprang durch die Pfützen und machte sich auf den Weg zur Bushaltestelle. Der Bus kam pünktlich und hielt gegenüber dem Pflegeheim an. Ein Krankenwagen stand vor dem Pflegeheim, und zwei Sanitäter fuhren ein Bett durch die offenen Türen. Katy folgte die Sanitätern.

„Ah, Katy", sagte die Schwester, „Dawn und ich werden Frau Goldmann in ihr Zimmer bringen. Könnten Sie bitte diese Plastiktüte mit der schmutzigen Wäsche in den Hauswirtschaftraum bringen und alles Essbare in den Mülleimer bitte werfen. Ich denke, dass Frau Goldmann nicht bald bereit sein wird zu essen. Sie sieht schrecklich aus, sie ging mit einer Infektion ins Krankenhaus, aber sie ist zurückgekommen, es geht ihr schlechter als zuvor. Die Schwester fühlte Frau Goldmanns Stirn. „Ich denke, dass sie Fieber hat. Ich rufe den Arzt später an. Danke Katy."

Katy hat die Plastiktüte abgeholt. Die Wäsche war sehr schmutzig und sie brachte sie in den Allzweckraum. Es gibt auch eine Kiste „Turkish Delight", einige Schokolade und auch einige Trauben. „Hmm", sagte Katy zu sich „Diese Sachen sind zu gut, um sie zu verschwenden. Nana wird diese ‚Turkish Delight' lieben, auch die Schokolade. Frau Goldmann hat nur die weichen Zentren gegessen.

Als Katy in Nanas Wohnung kam, sah sie, dass Nana mit ihrer

Gehhilfe rumläuft. „Hi Nana, ich habe dir einige ‚Turkish Delight' und Schokolade aus meiner Arbeit mitgebracht." „Danke", sagte Nana. Sie legte ein Stück Schokolade in ihren Mund „Pralinen, ich liebe diese Schokolade. Du gehst schon, Katy? Lebewohl!"

Zu Haus sagte Katy: „Mam, ich habe ein paar Trauben mitgebracht, weil einer der alten Leute fühlte sich nicht so gut. Ich dachte, es war schade, sie zu verschwenden. Mam sagte: „Wunderschön. Ich esse sie während ich ‚Coronation Street' sehe".

Die nächste Woche war sehr beschäftigt in dem Pflegeheim. Dawn war krank mit Kopfweh und musste nach Hause gehen . Frau Goldmann verschlechterte sich, Herr Clarke aus Raum 2 fühlte sich „dodgy". Katy wurde gebeten mehr zu helfen, der Besitzer des Pflegeheims versuchte mehr Pflegerinnen zu bekommen. Katy war aufgebracht und geschockt zu erfahren, dass Frau Goldmann nicht mehr lange leben würde und dachte, wie glücklich Nana war in ihrer gemütlichen Wohnung mit Hilfe einer Pflegerin. Als Katy nach Haus kam, sagte Rhodri: „Mam ist im Bett, Katy, sie hat schlimme Kopfschmerzen, wir werden Fisch und Chips zum Abendessen haben. Oh, und Katy, die Pflegerin hat angerufen. Nana hat eine erhöhte Temperatur, die Pflegerin hat den Arzt angerufen. Mam sagte, du sollst die Pflegerin anrufen." Katy antwortete: „Ok, Rhodri, ich hole den Fisch und Chips zuerst, dann rufe ich die Pflegerin an, bleibst du hier, Rhodri, und passt auf Mam auf. Wenn wir unser Abendessen gegessen haben, können wir einige Trauben und Käse essen. Ich habe sie von der Arbeit mitgebracht. Herr Clarke wollte sie nicht. Wir essen sie während wir Fernsehen sehen."

Jean's home language is English.

Escapemos

Anna Walsh

Sentada en el campo miro todo, escucho todo y siento todo. Hay tantos ruidos a la vez que no me puedo centrar en uno solo. Oigo el agudo canto de los pajaritos, el susurro de algo en las hojas tumbadas en el suelo del bosque, y algunos pájaros más discutiendo sobre lo que van a comer esta tarde. El sol brilla a través del follaje y el reflejo de la luz alumbra las flores silvestres. El vivo verde del césped contrasta con el desteñido color de las rocas que forman lo que queda de un gran monasterio. Imagino la simplicidad de la vida de los monjes que vivían en esta tierra hace siglos. Así que construyo las paredes altas y fuertes, y luego añado las vibrantes vidrieras y la imponente puerta de roble. Borro al hombre paseando a su perro y después de parpadear, estoy en el año 1177.

Un monje sale a recoger agua del pozo, que está fresca, pura y fría. Con su larga sotana negra y su cruz colgada del cuello, anda con determinación. Pasa por el río, donde los cisnes se arreglan de manera impecable. Extienden sus alas y sus plumas parecen tan suaves como nubes. Luego se van a pavonearse por su propia pasarela, mientras los patitos se lanzan al agua como niños y la sabia grulla vigila todo y a todos, como un guardián callado. El monje mete el cubo dentro del pozo y el viento deja salir un aullido chocante. El cielo se pone gris y pesado con rabia. La suave brisa se vuelve cargada de angustia. La corriente del río está trastornada y de repente, un barco de vikingos atraca a la orilla y unos hombres asquerosos con barba y barriga invaden el monasterio. El monje suelta el cubo sin pensar y corre tan rápido como una oveja arrinconada. Mira hacia el oscuro edificio y ve el fuego rugiendo por las ventanas. Las llamas feroces hacen que los monjes débiles y tímidos se dispersen como pollos sin cabeza, y parece que todos están desesperados.

Había una vez paz, tranquilidad y normalidad. Ahora todo el mundo está asustado, confundido y cada vez más molesto. Visualizo las tristes caras de los pobres monjes y miro las ruinas de lo que antes era una tremenda torre de calma. El viento me da una leve caricia en la mejilla, como para decirme que tenga fe y todo saldrá bien. Por el momento está lloviendo, pero al mal tiempo, buena cara.

Anna's home language is English.

L'hôtel de la mort

Joseph Young

1926. Two young English students were driving through a small village in France on a dark rainy night.

Passing the local police station on the left, they arrive at a hotel, an ancient building with raggedy windows and accompanying shutters with white, cracked paint. The students entered the hotel. The first one, a man around 20, medium build, dark hair with a reserved expression, followed closely by a small man, slightly younger, scrawny build with a dim-witted expression. The two men were greeted at the desk by the hotel lobbyist, a tall man sporting a straggly goatee with grey lifeless eyes looking over a pair of spectacles. 'Err nous avons… une reservation, John Yates et Daniel Acker,' the first student said unconvincingly. The lobbyist looked down at the papers in front of him, dead silent with the only sound being the storm outside. On the wall behind the lobbyist there was a large oil painting of a middle aged man with a thick moustache in a soldier's uniform. 'Who's the foot-slogger?' The scrawny man sniggered.

'Shut up Danny' uttered the older student impatiently.

'He was the owner of the hotel, the portrait was taken after the war in which he served, the lobbyist looked up and explained in a thick French accent. 'Your rooms are down the corridor.'

They walked down the dust stained corridor passing a large lounge containing a handful of people, all of whom were old and more dead than alive, sitting around a grand burning fireplace. One guest in particular drew Danny's attention. A small skeleton of a woman who looked as if her skin had been stretched over her bones with yellow rotten teeth and black eyes.

'Fucking hell,' Danny whispered to John as they walked to their rooms, 'there's no way I'm staying here.'

'What do you suppose we do, it's the middle of the night?' John replied, tired and clearly wanting to go to bed.

'I dunno but this place is freaking me out.'

'Look it'll be okay for one night then we can drive back into the village and find somewhere else.'

It was now almost dawn, Danny woke up startled, gasping for air and greeted by a putrid smell. Flustered and sweating he went to the adjoining bathroom and splashed cold water on his face, but when he looked up into the mirror he saw his face and hands dripping with blood. 'JOHNNY!' he yelled.

John was startled by his friend's screams and ran across the corridor into Danny's room only to see his friend's body lying on the bathroom floor in a pool of blood. 'What the…' John gasped. Turning around he sprinted desperately out of the hotel and down the road into the village to the police station. 'Aidez! Aidez-moi! Quelque chose de terrible… A l'hôtel de la mort,' he cried out at the befuddled gendarme, who replied 'Quel hôtel? The owner burned that hotel to the ground with him inside eight years ago after he went mad.'

Joseph's home language is English.

La realización personal

Alycia Holiday

At the start, I used to track the days by the exercise ring on my watch but that soon faded out. Week 1: «¡Yo me voy a poner tannnnn delgada!». Week 5: «¿Cuándo es la próxima comida para llevar?». I soon realised I do the same inside as I do outside. I cannot stay forced on one thing for more than five minutes. I constantly tell myself I am not doing enough, achieving enough, making the most of my time. «¿Qué has estado haciendo? ¿Cuál es el plan? ¿Cuál es el horario?».

I have learnt that your 85-year-old aunty can bring her awkwardness to any situation; she never goes out. Yet, she is now kicking off to get out of the house because she, all of a sudden, needs a new bra right away, even though you told her M&S for sure are not measuring people at the moment. There is nothing like shouting this at her front door. «No sé por qué ella no se pone los audífonos. Ella está completamente compos mentis. Al menos ahora todos en la calle saben que ella va sin tirantes y las lleva colgando». I have learnt it is possible to get through a full tv show box set in 72 hours if you tell yourself it's for 'research'. «Tres temporadas de La casa de papel, oh, me ayudará con mi español, ¿sí?». I have finally watched movies that, when people ask, they go: "WHAT? You have never seen that classic!". «Yo no estoy mal, solo soy así». I have hung out with my brother like we used to, wound him up like if we were kids. I have spent hours with old school friends talking about old times till early hours of the morning, often ending up with a pretty rough hangover. «Oh, por favor, no vuelvas a contar esa historia». I have daydreamt; I have been around the world but never left the house. «Wow, segundo Emmy de la noche, solo quiero agradecer a la academia esta oportunidad». I have sat and thought about things I have blocked out for years. I have changed what I want to do in life about twenty times, but always come back to the same thing: «No quiero estar atrapada en esta ciudad». I have cried, panicked and laughed to the point of stomach ache.

As more time passes, I have realised that maybe it is okay just to sit sometimes, «está bien no hacer nada a veces, solo detente». And, as you wait for things to go back to normal, you think «¿tal vez tu normalidad no es tan emocionante y a lo que no quieres volver tampoco? ¿Que habías perdido algo pero ahora te das cuenta y estás tratando de recuperarlo? ¿Tal vez estar tan asustada será ese empujón necesario?»

Sometimes it seems like your thoughts are in a different language, not something you are familiar with, but they make more sense than ever before. In the end you just hope that someone, even just one person, gets what you are saying. Even if it is just a snippet of the odd words, but it's enough to know that what you are thinking and saying makes sense.

Alycia's home language is English.

Lecker-bones

Layna Sadler

Forty kin ago, Syrah Nath flailed screekin thru da air-thin in da iron-hull an hands-laid a stake-claim on dis rock-bare. On da way, da iron-hull sundered one o da moons an sent er spinnin to make da Rings. Rings smile on us, star-up, star-down. An juss like Syrah, me brotherkin Tan screeked da ice, but for him screekin was a-colded unlike da scaldered iron o Syrah's Sky-flail. Him blade-hollowes screeked lightnin thru da ice-ways, thunderin ova da valis an skarin da Lawman outa-bed. Him shake-fist at da rock-bare, thinkin da valis got to crumblin again, but was juss Tan icin ova da ways all-afta.

Thaw an freeze, thaw an freeze, clock-ticked da spin, til Tan's Summer a-come an him got thirteened. Mam an Pap says Tan muss lumble wit him tings to High-here, so him come down be-braved. Him take da long-arm an da bangs an slep in a high-hole til freeze a-come. Ay watch da clock-ticks for thirty spins. Mam an Pap seems to unremember. Me-thinks Mam an Pap unremember me when Aym thirteened an get gone in da High-here slepin in a hole. Me inside-ticks hum for Tan, thrumblin-an-jumpskin in da black. One mid-dark sees me jumpskin cuz o long-arm bangs. Ay sees Tan flailin rock-ward, heyd all sundered. Then Ay comes to eyes-wide outa-bed.

Freeze a-come an Tan slanters-lumbles thru da mods all sklimmed an gangled. But not be-braved says Pap. Him an Mam gets to heyd-high-holdin spin to spin, like Tan got unremembered. Gamma says brotherkins gota bring lecker-bones from da High-here for we to gnaw, kep da growlers inside smilin, says all da bangs sit cozy in da long-arm still. Ay care not for lecker-bones. All Ay care for is Tan an da smilin Rings lookin down on him like Syrah, rememberin.

Come mid-freeze, Mam an Pap's a-cursin Tan on him cozy-bangs an lecker-bones runnin rown all wick an fleet in da High-here. Seems da growlers inside care for lecker-bones all-afta. Ayl get to icin an stingin da flickerfins, says Tan, an him tangle on blades, sharpin da hollowes. Ay followes afta.

But twenty clock-ticks afta an him stop icin da ways. Ay scrumbles to get along-him. Tan turns him heyd-flaps to da ice-ways an Ay sees a small ball-bellied kindlin playin wit him dolls. Da ice begins to screek an da lightnin skerch all da ways, thunderin thru da valis. Get off da ice-ways, says Tan, or youz get unremembered. But da kindlin sticks to playin.

Da lightnin gets to screekin.

Da kindlin sticks still.

Ay scrumbles to da valis rock. Da lightnin sunders da ice unda da kindlin an Tan drops him flickerfin-stick an stings, gets to icin wick an fleet to da hole.

Tan gets long-colded unda. Da clock-ticks sunder me insides. Da Rings stop smilin. Mid-bright lasts spin afta spin, til da kindlin gets flailed outa da hole like a flickerfin on a sting an Tan followes.

Tan got be-braved like Syrah Nath, Ay says, but him never tell Mam an Pap.

An da Rings stick to smilin, rememberin.

Layna's home language is English.

Afterword

We were inspired to undertake this project by the work that the teacher Giuseppe Rosa carried out with his fourth grade pupils at Scuola Primaria A. Diaz in Gessate, Italy, published under the title 'Il Decameron ai tempi del coronavirus'.

Printed in Great Britain
by Amazon

51439305R00161